What last year's readers said about the ALMANAK

'It lasted all the year round'
Mrs Cirrus, Tenth Egg Street, Ankh-Morpork

'My prospects improved no end by following the advice
set in this wonderful publication'
Prisoner 1784, The Tanty

'No end of fun, and useful also, especially afterwards'
Mr & Mrs name and address withheld

'Both absorbing and absorbent'
Mr Sproket, no fixed abode

'The article on wowhawks was very good, and the rest soaked up the blood very well'
Mr H., Lancre Castle

'Why?' Commander Vimes, City Watch

AMAZING, BUT TRUE.
Facts that will amaze & entertain you and your friends

The world's biggest Figgin
Baked at the Maple Leaf Café in Wincanton, Somerset. May 2004.
12 inches × 10 inches × 16 inches × 3½ inches deep.
It weighed over 2lb and was cut into 143 portions and fed to the
poor of the parish.

Last year's most spectacular landing
Mr Arnold Spend, a window cleaner, fell 65ft from the side of the Patrician's Palace
in Ankh-Morpork. He landed first on a passing wagon full of mattresses, in
Widdershins Broadway, then on a man selling balloons and fool's bladders in God
Street Alley, then on to a trampoline in the Fools' Guild. Celebrating his lucky escape
with a drink that night, he choked to death on a pickled egg. Amazing but true.

The biggest Brassica of Ankh-Morpork
Mr W. of Limping Lane off Grunefair, Ankh-Morpork, grew a Micklegreens Juicy to
a size of 25lb.
Yet he and his wife, Mabel, don't eat cabbages, only their cat does. Amazing but true.

An Amazing stroke of Luck
Master B. of Twitcher Street lost a Doldrum silver size 4 pin at the Lobbin Clout Pin
Market last February, and found a rare Tweedsmill hand-made pin the same day in
Ettercap Street. It fetched nearly $80.00 at auction, but he lost it all on the way home.
Amazing but true.

Make the Hole here

The Celebrated
DISCWORLD
Almanak
for

THE YEAR OF THE PRAWN

BEING AN ESSENTIAL GUIDE TO ALL ASPECTS OF LIFE, AND A RELIABLE MEANS OF ENSURING FERTILITY OF CROPS & LIVESTOCK. ALSO A BOON COMPANION IN AFFAIRS OF THE HEART & HEALTH.

WITH NOTES ON HUSBANDRY, PHYSIC, FAIRS & MARTS, AND OTHER SUCH INFORMATION AS WILL RENDER THIS PUBLICATION A STAUNCH COMPANION TO TOWNSMAN & TILLER OF THE SOIL ALIKE.

For the City of
ANKH-MORPORK
& surrounding Areas & Benefices

This *Almanak* is laid before you with the profound hope that it may not just ease the burden of Uncertainty that confounds man's progress through life, but it may also dispel that melancholy mantle which all too frequently shrouds our existence, namely the Fear of the Future.

The Unknown Future is held like a jewel in a rock, unseen to any but the most experienced prospector. Yet the God of The Orbs and Geometries has secreted, as it were, some clues as might a cook hide baubles in a Hogswatch pudding. It is the fate of the True Adept to brave mountain and storm to wrench the precious gem from its calcic tomb. Only then, dear reader, can the future be seen gleaming like a sixpence in a chimneysweep's earhole.

This process is not within the realm of Wizard or Witch, no matter how experienced they be at scrying or Necromancy. No mere Crystal Ball can measure the Stars' Passage across the firmament, or chart the endless perambulation of the Houses of the Night.

Only the True Astrologer has the key, the knowledge and the imagination even, to map the future. Like an explorer in a dark jungle, he must brave many dangers to win the wisdom that will bring enlightenment to all,

There is also much in this *Almanak* that will prove beneficial to those employed in matters agricultural. The Stars here play their essential part, and that knowledge unselfishly alloyed to the mundane arts of husbandry and wifery will be an undoubted benefit to all who heed the wisdom herein.

Those whose livelihood takes them into our Great Metropolis to earn their Fame and Fortune are not neglected. Our *Almanak* also furnishes them with such Astrological information as will render, with the aid of the Stars, any aspect of commerce or trade a path to Fortune and Prosperity.

Our Mortal Frame and Physical Well Being are also much influenced by the Celestial Realms. As Tide ebbs and flows, as seasons advance and retreat, so too does our Dyscly Body react to the Stars.

Many lifetimes of dedicated study have been devoted to this subject and within these pages you will find much that will prove most efficacious in the treatment of many of the ills that it is the lot of Man & Beast to suffer.

To those ends I commend this publication to you. May it be indeed the staff on which you lean. And may the benefits that shall undoubtedly issue from its careful study reflect on your perception and prudence in purchasing this *Almanak*.

But wait, for that is not all.

One does not need very fine arts of divination to know that, out in the rural districts, where paper is rarely seen, the *Almanak* has a special place in people's hearts and, eventually, elsewhere. We are not proud. All are consumed by the great Wheels of Time and Space, and our humble book is no exception. Regular readers will, therefore, note that this year we have printed a special hole where the string may be inserted.

he who sees All,
but knows when not to look

Memo From Ronald Goatberger, publisher
To: Thomas Cropper, overseer

Dear Mr Cropper,
As you know, I will be running the company while my uncle is unwell and may I say it is a great privilege. I did explain to him that I know nothing about how publishing works but he said no one knows how publishing works, and knowing anything only slows you down and gets in the way. However, I am afraid I do not understand the import of the last paragraph of the frontispiece. Can you enlighten me, please?

Memo to Ronald Goatberger
From: Thomas Cropper, overseer

Yes, sir. People hang the Almanak in the privy. For use as and when, you might say. I'm told they're much relieved when the new edition comes out.

Memo From Ronald Goatberger, publisher
To: Thomas Cropper, overseer

The privy? But this is the distilled wisdom of the ages!

Memo to Ronald Goatberger

From: Thomas Cropper, overseer

Well, sir, in the Wisdom of the Ages business, sir, I always used to tell your uncle it helps if you can have a good laugh.

 Make the Hole here

This be for the
COMMON YEAR

That being the 400 days that measure the season from Winter's Edge until the snows come again and Hogswatch is celebrated.

All Celestial Measurements, Observations, and notations of Stars, Houses of the Firmament, and other divers Heavenly Bodies are taken on the Full Celestial Year, of 800 days, which encompasses 2 common years.

All Mathematical formulae & arcane observations are made in strict accordance with the precepts & guidance of the masters of the law in
The Unseen University of Ankh-Morpork
and the
Royal Observatory of Krull.

AT THE START OF
THIS SEASON
being known as
the Common Year 2005
Scholar's Year 1657
&
THE YEAR OF THE PRAWN,
THE SUN
RISES LEFT
AS I FACE THE HUB

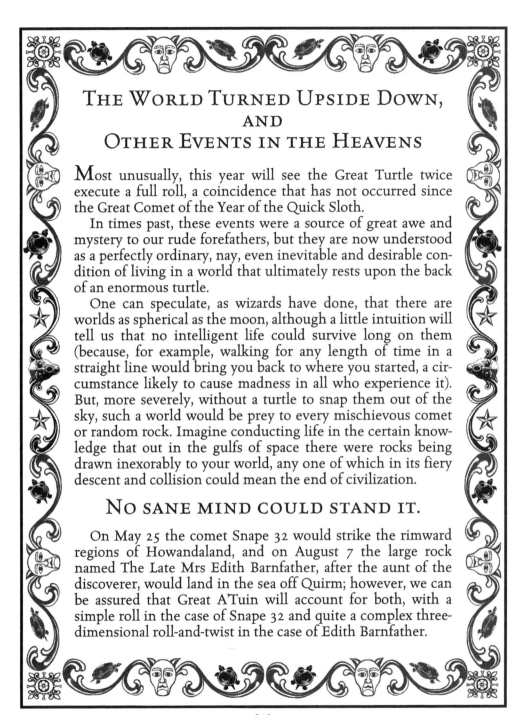

The World Turned Upside Down,
and
Other Events in the Heavens

Most unusually, this year will see the Great Turtle twice execute a full roll, a coincidence that has not occurred since the Great Comet of the Year of the Quick Sloth.

In times past, these events were a source of great awe and mystery to our rude forefathers, but they are now understood as a perfectly ordinary, nay, even inevitable and desirable condition of living in a world that ultimately rests upon the back of an enormous turtle.

One can speculate, as wizards have done, that there are worlds as spherical as the moon, although a little intuition will tell us that no intelligent life could survive long on them (because, for example, walking for any length of time in a straight line would bring you back to where you started, a circumstance likely to cause madness in all who experience it). But, more severely, without a turtle to snap them out of the sky, such a world would be prey to every mischievous comet or random rock. Imagine conducting life in the certain knowledge that out in the gulfs of space there were rocks being drawn inexorably to your world, any one of which in its fiery descent and collision could mean the end of civilization.

No sane mind could stand it.

On May 25 the comet Snape 32 would strike the rimward regions of Howandaland, and on August 7 the large rock named The Late Mrs Edith Barnfather, after the aunt of the discoverer, would land in the sea off Quirm; however, we can be assured that Great A'Tuin will account for both, with a simple roll in the case of Snape 32 and quite a complex three-dimensional roll-and-twist in the case of Edith Barnfather.

DO NOT BE AFEARED

('afeared' being far worse than being afraid!)

FOR THE TURTLE WILL PREVAIL!

The oceans will not slosh!
Mighty towers will not topple!
Be secure in the knowledge that the world will travel as one!

However, it may be a good idea to take the more precious items of china off the shelves.

For several days you will see the heavens move, and marvel at skies not usually seen, because a benevolent Creator has seen fit to put stars even in places where we don't usually see them, and also keeps them on in daytime. We expect on August 3 to witness a Turtle Eclipse of the Sun as one of the mighty flippers, beating the aether with extra force in order to begin the roll, briefly rises above the Rim, and people who tend towards vertigo or seasickness would be well advised to stay indoors at night time, particularly on August 6 when the stars will be moving quite strongly.

Your questions answered!

'WILL I NEED TO WEAR DARK GLASSES TO VIEW THE ROLL?'

ANSWER: ONLY IF YOU FEEL THE NEED TO WEAR DARK GLASSES AT NIGHT. MANY PEOPLE DO, ESPECIALLY IN THE COOLER AREAS.

'WILL THERE BE LOUD NOISES?'

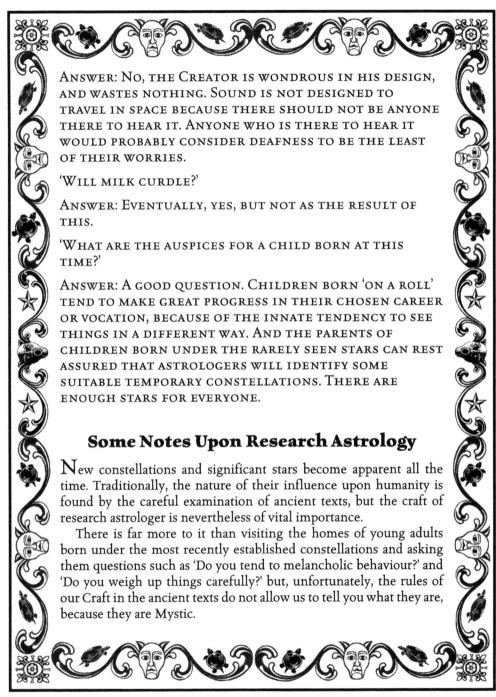

ANSWER: NO, THE CREATOR IS WONDROUS IN HIS DESIGN, AND WASTES NOTHING. SOUND IS NOT DESIGNED TO TRAVEL IN SPACE BECAUSE THERE SHOULD NOT BE ANYONE THERE TO HEAR IT. ANYONE WHO IS THERE TO HEAR IT WOULD PROBABLY CONSIDER DEAFNESS TO BE THE LEAST OF THEIR WORRIES.

'WILL MILK CURDLE?'

ANSWER: EVENTUALLY, YES, BUT NOT AS THE RESULT OF THIS.

'WHAT ARE THE AUSPICES FOR A CHILD BORN AT THIS TIME?'

ANSWER: A GOOD QUESTION. CHILDREN BORN 'ON A ROLL' TEND TO MAKE GREAT PROGRESS IN THEIR CHOSEN CAREER OR VOCATION, BECAUSE OF THE INNATE TENDENCY TO SEE THINGS IN A DIFFERENT WAY. AND THE PARENTS OF CHILDREN BORN UNDER THE RARELY SEEN STARS CAN REST ASSURED THAT ASTROLOGERS WILL IDENTIFY SOME SUITABLE TEMPORARY CONSTELLATIONS. THERE ARE ENOUGH STARS FOR EVERYONE.

Some Notes Upon Research Astrology

New constellations and significant stars become apparent all the time. Traditionally, the nature of their influence upon humanity is found by the careful examination of ancient texts, but the craft of research astrologer is nevertheless of vital importance.

There is far more to it than visiting the homes of young adults born under the most recently established constellations and asking them questions such as 'Do you tend to melancholic behaviour?' and 'Do you weigh up things carefully?' but, unfortunately, the rules of our Craft in the ancient texts do not allow us to tell you what they are, because they are Mystic.

AS ABOVE, SO BELOW

Never was this ancient precept more aptly demonstrated than by the discovery, last year, of a lady whom we shall call Mrs Grace Breadalbin, who is as far as is known the only person on whom the ancient tides of astronomy work counter to the normal procedures. This is to say, everything she does affects the universe.

This came to light only by accident, when she slipped on the stairs and two stars collided. Subsequently, examination of her diaries indicated that there is a partial eclipse of the sun every time she visits her sister in Quirm, and when she does her washing it rains. Most people believe this happens to everyone, which was why she hadn't realized that there was anything unusual in her case. In addition, summer time arrives when she airs her summer wardrobe, and winter turns up shortly after she buys a new coat; Mrs Breadalbin had put this down simply to being well prepared.

Since the universe had been going for some time prior to the birth of the lady, it is assumed that she is only one of a long line of people, or creatures, who have serially occupied this role.

After examining the ancient texts, the Guild of Astrologers have advised Mrs Breadalbin to go on as normal but on no account to a) take up tennis, b) mix up her wardrobes or c) wear anything with blue roses on it.

The tentative experiments that led to these conclusions were undertaken during the freak gale and unexpected meteor shower last July.

While it is believed that her case is very rare, it is really only an extreme version of our normal human tendency to change the universe in our immediate vicinity. People should not be alarmed. Readers who believe that everything they do affects objects billions of miles away of whose very existence they are unaware should sit quietly and have an emergency astrologer sent for, who will explain to them that this is very unlikely to be the case because in fact it works the other way around.

1	OCTEDAY	🌙
2	MONDAY	
3	TUESDAY	
4	WEDNESDAY	
5	THURSDAY	
6	FRIDAY	
7	SATURDAY	
8	SUNDAY	
9	OCTEDAY	
10	MONDAY	
11	TUESDAY	
12	WEDNESDAY	
13	THURSDAY	
14	FRIDAY	
15	SATURDAY	
16	SUNDAY	●

ICK, the month no year will own.

In this month shall be the fall of a great House in Klatch. A man whose Number is Two will lose a great fortune or win one. There will be a swarm of locusts in Hersheba, slackening off towards the end of the month with outbreaks of frogs. In the forests of Lancre a tree shall walk though no man or woman shall witness this. There will be much lamentation in Borogravia. In the red land of Fourecks there will be drought, and a rain of small items, but *Nullus Anxietas*.

Into this month all the true nature of winter is poured. Oh, we will illustrate Winter with pictures of snow and glittering trees, but Ick brings Winter in all its dreadful reality, viz, sleet and iron skies and mud alternating with killing frosts.

Ick

Clear yard and byre of dung while the frosts be hard. Do not let them crust. There is nothing worse than one boot being sucked off a farmer's foot by the suppurating mass of a deeply filled yard, unless it be the look upon his face as he realizes that the boot is now lost to the stinking mass and he will have to put his stockinged foot down somewhere…

Clean thy Dovecot: but leave a bastion of droppings around the hole to protect new eggs and the first hatching against the icy blast. In truth, anyone who marvels at the cooing of doves should see their nest sometimes and gain much cynical wisdom thereof.

Leave from trapping Conies and Dove, let Doe go to buck. Nature is making Increase. You would not wish to be shot at, at a time like this, treat others likewise.

Set Runcible Pease, but not too shallow, and never when the moon is waning, otherwise they will grow into snakes. Now is a good time also to make decking, which will be required in the garden later.

Prune such trees as do give fruit and pollard those that give stave and hurdle and, with luck, decking. Spare such Mistle & Ivy as sheep do find wholesome.

If you have reason to believe the rams got out early, now is the time to prepare the lambing shed. And, if you keep sheep where the Nac Mac Feegle are found, you will do well to leave a small offering there for them, such as a bottle of whisky and perhaps the cooked stomach of a sheep stuffed with other sheep's stomachs. A little kindness to the 'wee people' now is much better than being nutted in the ankles later.

Just because the sun's shining doesn't mean it's not raining somewhere.

Old Proverb

1	OCTEDAY	
2	MONDAY	
3	TUESDAY	
4	WEDNESDAY	
5	THURSDAY	
6	FRIDAY	
7	SATURDAY	
8	SUNDAY	
9	OCTEDAY	
10	MONDAY	
11	TUESDAY	●
12	WEDNESDAY	
13	THURSDAY	
14	FRIDAY	
15	SATURDAY	
16	SUNDAY	
17	OCTEDAY	
18	MONDAY	
19	TUESDAY	
20	WEDNESDAY	
21	THURSDAY	
22	FRIDAY	
23	SATURDAY	
24	SUNDAY	
25	OCTEDAY	☾
26	MONDAY	
27	TUESDAY	
28	WEDNESDAY	
29	THURSDAY	
30	FRIDAY	
31	SATURDAY	
32	SUNDAY	

✶ OFFLE ✶

Of the Common Year being the First Month, in the First house, that being The house of Io.

Great Kings will count their wealth, and Potentates plot to increase their domain. A time of landslides, and talk of landslides, and talk that cannot be heard because of the landslide going past. There will be a plague in hergen, and lamentation. There will be a procession of beggars in Tsort, led by a dancing Goat. A Fish will talk in riddles, which will amaze the high Priests of Djelibeybi.

In this month in the Year of Two Cats a farm in the steep country above NoThingFjord slid downhill and landed upon the farm below, causing each farmer to sue the other for trespass.

A good time for the birthing of Livestock, as the COW OF HEAVEN is in this house.

Being a time of Ice, Silver is the metal of Luck.

The KNOTTED STRING is ascending, so Trade Transactions are well favoured for those who carry a knotted string about their person.

The CELESTIAL PARSNIP still ensures the frosts will be harsh, but that be good news for Dung Merchants and Carters.

Winter strikes cold, so children under the age of ten years should be covered in goose fat and brown paper and sewn into their clothing, which will keep them warm and snug until the balmy breezes of Spring.

AT THIS TIME, THE PRUDENT HUSBANDMAN WILL LOOK TO HIS SHED, WHEREIN HE WILL, IF WILY, HAVE SECRETED A COMFY CHAIR AND A SUPPLY OF GOOD ALE, AND TOBACCO TOO IF HE IS SO MINDED.

Offle

This can be another hard month.

Like the mighty dung beetle of Hersheba which can roll a cubit of dung for a mile or more, so you must now emulate that industrious insect and gather that which has been collected from byre and yard, and cart it to that place where you have decided the heap shall be. By doing so now the cart wheels will do no harm to grass or road, and such smell as there is will not be too aggravating.

Dig Garden and destroy Mallow and other such malicious tines.

Set Runcible Pease.

A time of Bargaining and invitation to Trade, for those who deal and barter will be short of a bob or two. Though wear of the thermal john the long with cosy gusset, and big thick socks, for 'tis the man whose parts are frosted most counts the pennies towards a mulled ale.

Prepare the Lambing shed; get in liniment and plenty of turpentine.

If a fine pig be sought for the Soul Cake Day, then give over the finest of the litter to the housewife to rear.

> Red be a singular good colour this Month.
> Much comfort can be found in Mulled Cider.
> Be wary of men selling fish, or fish shaped items.
> Lucky Vegetable: Swede.

Men were born to trouble as the sparks fly upwards, and should endeavour to create heavier sparks. Old Proverb

1	OCTEDAY	
2	MONDAY	
3	TUESDAY	
4	WEDNESDAY	
5	THURSDAY	
6	FRIDAY	
7	SATURDAY	
8	SUNDAY	
9	OCTEDAY	
10	MONDAY	
11	TUESDAY	
12	WEDNESDAY	
13	THURSDAY	
14	FRIDAY	
15	SATURDAY	
16	SUNDAY	
17	OCTEDAY	
18	MONDAY	
19	TUESDAY	
20	WEDNESDAY	
21	THURSDAY	●
22	FRIDAY	
23	SATURDAY	
24	SUNDAY	
25	OCTEDAY	
26	MONDAY	
27	TUESDAY	
28	WEDNESDAY	
29	THURSDAY	
30	FRIDAY	
31	SATURDAY	
32	SUNDAY	

✳ FEBRUARY ✳

Of the Common Year being the Second month, in the First house, that being, The house of Io.

Winter in hard grasp does grip the land. Poor and rich alike draw closer to the fire, but the rich will have larger fires. The old and infirm do slip away to the call of the Reaper, and this is the month where the most planting is done by the Sexton, and who knoweth where his crop may flourish.

The Knotted String and Celestial Parsnip are now predominant in this House, influencing from the heavens above the doings of men and cattle, although mostly the doings of men.

A two-headed beast shall be born in Lancre, but will excite no interest, for this happens quite a lot around Slice.

In the land of the D'regs a rain of fish, and they will say 'what are these things?' The mighty Ankh will freeze, and a great captain of men shall dance upon the ice.

Gird your self in Yellow where possible.

February

Hard frosts do still render the land as iron, yet harrowing can be done, and all crops do benefit greatly from it.

Be careful though when hoeing amongst the reannuals, as a garden implement from next summer can cause a serious injury today.

Now is the time to plant toads; you will be glad of this later in the year, depend upon it. It is well known that toads grow underground, like potatoes. At this time, too, the cunning farmer will walk the ploughed fields looking for mother stones, those stones apparently made of many smaller stones bound together as in a pudding, and root them out so that they do not breed, for surely everyone has noticed how fresh stones appear after rain, in a field previously quite emptied of them. It is by Clear Observation such as this that culture may Progress, and not by rank superstition.

If the Swan be nesting high, then floods are expected; if only the head of the Swan may be seen, they have arrived abruptly. If their nests are within the branches of small trees, lay by some stilts and make a bed up in the loft.

This is a good time to set and mend all tools and equipment, a job that happily will require a man to be closeted for some considerable time in his Shed.

See closely to your clouts, and bare naught needlessly for the privy, for in truth 'tis still most dangerous to expose the parts.

1	Octeday	
2	Monday	☽
3	Tuesday	
4	Wednesday	
5	Thursday	
6	Friday	
7	Saturday	
8	Sunday	
9	Octeday	
10	Monday	
11	Tuesday	
12	Wednesday	
13	Thursday	
14	Friday	
15	Saturday	
16	Sunday	
17	Octeday	
18	Monday	
19	Tuesday	
20	Wednesday	
21	Thursday	
22	Friday	
23	Saturday	●
24	Sunday	
25	Octeday	
26	Monday	
27	Tuesday	
28	Wednesday	
29	Thursday	
30	Friday	
31	Saturday	
32	Sunday	

✳ March ✳

Of the Common Year.
Being the Third Month, in the
Second House.
The Gate being that House.

Mubbo the Hyena Stalks the Heavens and the Two Fat Cousins are abroad. The former denotes a threat, mostly to beasts, the latter a depredation to pantry or larder, and when conjoined they represent a time of some anxiety of provisioning.

The stars foretell a great storm over the Circle Sea, and the earth shall shake in Muntab. A great Sage will walk in Hergen, and an angry mule with a name like Parsley will savage the unwary of Vanglemesh. It will be a time of small hammers, but will seem otherwise. A man with three names shall achieve a strange reputation.

March

Abroad, this is the time of the dancing hare over the fields and the growth of lust amongst the common man, with luck and a running start. Commerce in Cities is heard like the chattering of Jays, and the men of money hear the sound of the loot.

But across the Plains of Sto the Cabbage song will be heard, as all who can walk, crawl, or stagger are out placing the young plants in their earthy beds to grow big and strong. At this time the workers in each village will elect from amongst themselves the Cabbage King, a skilled man who knows the wily ways of the brassica.

Now is a good time for the husbandman to consider the placing of the new Patio, which is not to be undertaken lightly, preferably never on a rising moon, and never in one weekend, when it will end up looking silly. The man of sense, mindful of the state of the heavens, will use slabs of one colour only.

Sap is rising, and when the moon be new it is a most Sovereign balm to use when grafting fruit trees. At this time, carry a live mouse in your pocket, for fear of bats.

If you harvested reannual crops last year – that is to say, those crops sown in areas of high natural magic that causeth them to grow backwards in time – then BEWARE and TAKE CARE that you sow them now. Let 'As you reap, so must you sow' be your motto here. Reaping then what you do not sow now can cause terrible calamities, not the least being that the food you ate then will no longer exist and therefore death by starvation, lashing back through the many worlds of Time, may claim you in an instant!

Set your potato tubers, there's good eating on them, and onions as well, for even in the town garden such may be grown providing the soil is well manured. Mulch your toads well, and discard any that sing. This is a time when a man be glad he sowed leeks last year, because they will have survived pigeon, rook, rabbit and slug, the reason being, nothing else in Creation wants to eat the damned things.

If the doorstep is scrubbed so will be the privy. Old Proverb

1	OCTEDAY	
2	MONDAY	☾
3	TUESDAY	
4	WEDNESDAY	
5	THURSDAY	
6	FRIDAY	
7	SATURDAY	
8	SUNDAY	
9	OCTEDAY	
10	MONDAY	
11	TUESDAY	
12	WEDNESDAY	
13	THURSDAY	
14	FRIDAY	●
15	SATURDAY	
16	SUNDAY	
17	OCTEDAY	
18	MONDAY	
19	TUESDAY	
20	WEDNESDAY	
21	THURSDAY	
22	FRIDAY	
23	SATURDAY	
24	SUNDAY	
25	OCTEDAY	
26	MONDAY	☽
27	TUESDAY	
28	WEDNESDAY	
29	THURSDAY	
30	FRIDAY	
31	SATURDAY	
32	SUNDAY	

✳ APRIL ✳

Of the Common Year. Being the Fourth month, Leaving the Second house and entering into the Third.

In Klatch, there will be a strange multiplication of camels. In Muntab, it will rain bedsteads, turning to chairs later. There will be rumours, and rumours of rumours, and men will say, what is this? A man associated with gloves shall make a strange discovery. In Borogravia there will be talk of war but women shall have the last word.

WEZEN is seen at the edge Rimward, and its influence shall be slight, giving only headaches to those who drink too deeply of strong beer.

The BULL doth rampage and snort, its breath making great clouds, which fall to earth as a rain full of great potency for all growing things, although others disagree. It would be wise not to venture into the Brown Islands, as a mighty Sea Dragon will arise nearby and devour all sea vessels – again.

Commerce is easier and markets better attended, and when sun does shine 'tis worth an extra penny on anything when selling.

April

All should be growing lush and green under the countenance of heaven. A time of growing for some, but not for the bulls, boars, and rams, of whom some needs must be for the unkind gelding knife, yet even this is better than the two bricks method, which was very bad for the farmer's fingers.

But not all is merrymaking – not for the rams and bulls, for certain – and hard work behind the plough is called for. Fences need repairing, and the winter dung can be spread. Those readers in Ankh-Morpork would do well to buy their compost from Mr H. King, which will have rotted down to a fine mulch leaving no trace of the original material, be it weeds, kitchen wastes or dead dogs, to name not the worst.

Sheep can be put up on the downlands, or, in special cases, down on the uplands.

The beekeeper should choose a fine day to inspect his or her bees, feeding them small amounts of beef and cheese to strengthen them. Bees, as is well known, should be told everything that is going on in the household, for fear that otherwise they will fly indoors to find out for themselves.

If you live in the rural districts, especially in the Ramtop Mountains, you may find a witch visiting just at the moment when you are opening your beehive. If you would like a season of quiet bees, who swarm conveniently and work industriously, then there is no finer investment now than to give her several jars of the very best of last year's honey. Remember, you must talk to your bees, and your bees will talk to other bees, and those bees will talk to her bees … and a witch, while not saying much to her bees, listens to them all the time.

As the memory of winter now ebbs, all is bustle indoors and out. It must be remembered that the eye of the master makes the horse fat, and that of the mistress keeps house and dairy clean.

The good husbandman must now spend considerable time in his Shed. When quizzed by the mistress of the house as to what this task may be that must needs take so much time, he need only reply 'pricking out' in order to be left alone.

1	OCTEDAY	
2	MONDAY	
3	TUESDAY	
4	WEDNESDAY	
5	THURSDAY	
6	FRIDAY	
7	SATURDAY	
8	SUNDAY	
9	OCTEDAY	
10	MONDAY	●
11	TUESDAY	
12	WEDNESDAY	
13	THURSDAY	
14	FRIDAY	
15	SATURDAY	
16	SUNDAY	
17	OCTEDAY	
18	MONDAY	
19	TUESDAY	
20	WEDNESDAY	
21	THURSDAY	
22	FRIDAY	
23	SATURDAY	
24	SUNDAY	
25	OCTEDAY	
26	MONDAY	☾
27	TUESDAY	
28	WEDNESDAY	
29	THURSDAY	
30	FRIDAY	
31	SATURDAY	
32	SUNDAY	

✶ MAY ✶

Of the Common Year.
Being the Fifth Month of the Common Year, in the House of The Bull.

The Bull still rampages about this month, causing much growth and some commotion. We see the rising of Hast's Trumpet, and that conjoined with the said Bull doth make a celestial clamour. 'Tis a time not to make music on any instrument of brass, though wood be good if plucked. The mountains of the Blade in far off Kythia will move and shake; do not go there if ye be of a nervous disposition, though it will be a capital cure for constipation, but rhubarb is easier and available, if it has been forced.

The time of the Bull also turns the young to thoughts of an earthly nature, especially the male youth. Give them strong porridge in which the Senna Pod is crushed; 'twill take their minds from the laughing eyes of maidens and keep them very close to home.

May

Keep an eye out for caterpillars, especially the big hairy fat green ones as they will eat anything, even babies. However the Toads planted in February should now be making a showing, and will make a good meal of them, the one before the other.

Sow now your Barley and Oats, and hemp and flax if the ground be ready. 'Tis a capital time for garden and croft: there are few seeds that may not be put into the earth at this time. Turn your young cattle into the woodland and the young calves on to the grass, and to these and your sheep do administer a little salt twice a week to prevent Skroops. Look to your lambs: if the tails be active and they do greatly wriggle, then they may well have the Gripples. If the dung hangs to the wool much damage can be done, likely leading to Wooden-ness of the Gargets. Cut away the adhesions and anoint the luxations with tar, and, if maggots be present in the flesh, then wash them well with scab water, which is a strong decoction of tobacco stalks in chamber lye, and treat with turpentine.

Caterpillar nests can be found at this time by stalking the caterpillars carefully and following them home in the evenings.

Keep good watch for your bees, for now and in June they will want to swarm. Listen for the sound of the Queen: if she has sisters they will fight or fly.

IT IS A LAW OF NATURE THAT NO MAN MAY DENY, THAT A BEEKEEPER IN PURSUIT OF HIS SWARM MAY FOLLOW IT WHERESOEVER IT GOETH AND RECLAIM IT NO MATTER WHERE IT MAY PITCH. AND THUS IT WAS THAT, IN THE YEAR OF THREE HORSES, THE MAN LATER KNOWN AS HAROLD THE BEE-TAMER, ACCOMPANIED BY MEN HE CLAIMED WERE HIS APPRENTICE BEEKEEPERS, TRACKED A SWARM INTO THE STRONG ROOM OF THE MERCANTILE & COMMERCIAL BANK OF BAD HEISSE AND, AS WORRIED STAFF FLED THE STINGS, RECOVERED THE SWARM AND THREE HUNDREDWEIGHTS OF GOLD.

1	Octeday	
2	Monday	
3	Tuesday	
4	Wednesday	
5	Thursday	
6	Friday	
7	Saturday	
8	Sunday	
9	Octeday	
10	Monday	
11	Tuesday	
12	Wednesday	
13	Thursday	
14	Friday	
15	Saturday	
16	Sunday	
17	Octeday	
18	Monday	●
19	Tuesday	
20	Wednesday	
21	Thursday	
22	Friday	
23	Saturday	
24	Sunday	
25	Octeday	
26	Monday	
27	Tuesday	
28	Wednesday	
29	Thursday	
30	Friday	
31	Saturday	
32	Sunday	

✷ JUNE ✷

Of the Common Year.
Being the Sixth Month, and in the House of the Bull with the House of Melok in abeyance.

Cubal's Flame lights up the beginning of the month, Sandrit doth come to view in the midst, and Melok accompanies The House of The Bright Cabbage.

Much movement in the firmament, but little of note to afflict those below, save a possible inflammation of the skin to those of a fair complexion. 'Tis a mighty good time for merrymaking and the sun being close to midsky gives a long afternoon. The Melok, being a benign House, bodes well for all, especially those who congregate with swine of all types.

A mighty Dragon might be seen in Ecalpon, arising from the sea, with huge teeth large enough to crush any boat within its reach. Huge scaly wings could cause the beast to fly, and it may have breath like a thousand privies – again.

June

The shearing of sheep can now take place, but be wary of any injury caused by the shears, and treat accordingly as before. As with shearing the sheep, so with the produce of the land everything has its time for ripeness, and when it ought to be gathered for the best opportunity.

Hay making is now to be started. The grass and ground ought to be very dry before you begin to make hay; until such time employ yourself in the mending of barns, Summer fallowing, and other husbandly matters, so that when harvest time comes you will have nothing to do but tend to it.

In the garden or smallholding, the good husbandman will turn his mind to his water feature. Time was when all a man must needs do to have a reputation as a fine gardener was grow potatoes the size of his head and pumpkins big enough for a small family to live in, but now 'tis all changed and dainty and it is upon his flowering shrub and boulder-bestrewn 'water feature' that he is to be judged.

So nothing for it but to hie, or hoe, to the new garden centre which has replaced the seedsman's shop where once sinewy men who knew how to talk to owls dispensed red beans and hard pease in plain brown bags to men who gardened because their family must be fed. Here, somewhere behind the wind chimes from HungHung, the knitwear, the silk flowers and the barbecue sets, the good husbandman will buy a packet of seed for $2.99. When he reaches the counter, he will say thereupon to the man there the ancient saying of the gardener, thusly: 'Gordon Bennett, I remember when you could get a whole packet for a tanner'. And when he gets home he will find that the packet contains ten seeds.

Hay making shall be done if the weather is dry, hay-ho'ing if wet.

An alleyway's as good as a highway to a dying man.

Old Proverb

JUNE

This is the
Cabbage Month
on the Sto Plains

Who will not honour the cabbage, the sprout and the broccoli? Oh, people will talk about the potato in all its infinite variety, and the onion is not to be sneezed at, and the carrot has much to recommend it, but for year-round feeding you must eat your greens. And such greens!

Never have they been so celebrated as in the famous paintings of Josiah 'Cabbage' Remnant, and many farms on the plains have a print of his *Landscape With Cabbage* or the equally famous *Prospect of Sprouts Upon a February* or, perhaps, his masterpiece *Still Life with Cabbage, Broccoli both Green and Purple, Sprouts, Kale and Elderly Couple being Attacked by Werewolf.* (There is clearly a story attached to this picture, but the truth of it is not known.) It is for certain that the cabbage, which occupies most of the picture, was the prize-winning 'Rumptuous Javelin', which weighed 295lbs and made three barrels of coleslaw which were exhibited at the Scrote and District Agricultural and Domestic Show. The chimneys and occasional bits of house visible over the top of the monster cabbage have been positively identified as Rumptuous Hall, the home of Sir Henry and Lady Rumptuous who, it is also believed, are the small figures seen on the left of the picture cowering beside the ornamental fountain. Beyond that, little is clear. (It is understood that Josiah painted very fast and with total intent on his work, and apparently painted what he saw with, as it were, little actual interest in or involvement with it unless it was green.)

The cabbage is believed to have originated in the Agatean Empire, where in some areas breaking the wind loudly after meals was considered a compliment to the host. From there, it is thought, it was brought across the icecap and found its way to the Sto Plains, where probably the Agatean original can still be found in the small, dark cabbage known as the 'Burpy'. There are now no fewer than three hundred varieties of cabbage, for year-round gustatory delight.

Still Life with Cabbage, Broccoli both Green and Purple, Sprouts, Kale and Elderly Couple being Attacked by Werewolf, by Josiah Remnant.

A *great Curiosity* on the Sto Plains is the town of BIG CABBAGE, about one hundred miles hubwards of Ankh-Morpork. In the centre of the town and, indeed, the centre of the high road, so that carts must needs divert around it, is the *Big Cabbage*, which is artfully made of concrete painted green and white. It is hollow and will hold twenty seated people. Nearby are the *Museum of Caterpillars* and *Fun with Cabbagez!!*, an amusement centre for travellers tired after mayhap several days travelling through cabbage fields. The town has been burned down twice, and a good living is made by the townsfolk who fine visitors $5 for attacking the Big Cabbage with their bare hands. For some reason this usually happens after they have seen the menu at the only eating establishment in fifty miles, known as *Cabbage 'n' Sprouts*. Not to be missed, if you have a large enough weapon, is the *Cabbage Research Centre* just outside the town, where strange green lights are seen at night.

JUNE

While of course the cabbage harvest continues, as it does for most of the year, all hands must now to the new season's cabbage fields for the thinning and hoeing of the plants. This must be done well and with great diligence as the reputation of farm and family are judged by the splendour of this crop. The endless nature of this worthy work is noted in the famous song:

> **Cabbages in my garden grow,**
> **Cabbages in the fields do show,**
> **I must get out there with my hoe,**
> **Diligently tilling, row on row,**
> **But rather to the pub will go.**

The third Monday in the month is known as Squash Monday, when all able-bodied workers must once again hie to the fields (or hoe to the fields if in possession of a medical certificate) for the beginning of the caterpillar-squashing season. This will of course extend for a good six weeks, culminating in the public holiday of Nip Friday, when there will be fairs in every town and young men will compete against all comers in the caterpillar-squashing championships, using especially large caterpillars in a field which will have been saved for the occasion. The winner by tradition wins a new hat and a belt with a silver buckle, as well as the ancient title of Jack of the Green Fingers.

Make the Hole here

Whatever the crop may be, the secret of success in garden or field is, of course, WORMS. A trained team of worms under a skilful worm-piper can work wonders. The best are never cheap and personal recommendation is better than any advertisement, and the work they do in aerating the soil, digesting any little unwanted visitor or dead dog, is more than made up for in cost.

We no longer see the worm herds of former times, when drovers would drive up to five million worms from farm to farm. The very earth trembled underfoot and mounded up as they passed, and stout trees would be uprooted. They were rough and ready men, the drovers, with their wormskin belts and huge appetite for drink, but they are all now underground and at one with their herds, and the fertility of our soils is the worse for it. Only a few signs remain to mark their passing. Those of an antiquarian bent would do well to visit The Jolly Vermiculturalist on the road to Sto Lat, where there is on display an original worm prod and a small museum of worm memorabilia, entrance price 3p.

No cabbage is all heart.	Old Proverb

1	OCTEDAY	
2	MONDAY	
3	TUESDAY	
4	WEDNESDAY	☽
5	THURSDAY	
6	FRIDAY	
7	SATURDAY	
8	SUNDAY	
9	OCTEDAY	☉
10	MONDAY	
11	TUESDAY	
12	WEDNESDAY	
13	THURSDAY	
14	FRIDAY	
15	SATURDAY	
16	SUNDAY	
17	OCTEDAY	
18	MONDAY	
19	TUESDAY	
20	WEDNESDAY	
21	THURSDAY	
22	FRIDAY	
23	SATURDAY	
24	SUNDAY	
25	OCTEDAY	
26	MONDAY	
27	TUESDAY	
28	WEDNESDAY	●
29	THURSDAY	
30	FRIDAY	
31	SATURDAY	
32	SUNDAY	

✶ GRUNE ✶

Of the Common Year.
This being the time of change when the sun doth rise on the Right when facing the Hub.

Midsummer Day falls the day next after the 7th and Old Toesy is graced by Melok that very night. Vut the Evenstar beloved of lovers is to be in the influence later in the month, so all is well-starred for those of a romantic persuasion.

'Tis a most auspicious time for widows who finding the juices still stir do meet with widowers or bachelor farmers at the midsummer fairs that mark this month.

The harvest is yet to be gathered and a well-endowed helpmate is more use than a pretty widow to a man with 40 acres to get in, and hogs to fatten before the fall. A pretty face is all well and good, but what a man needs for his farm is a wife who can carry a pig under each arm.

☉ The Sun that rose Widdershins now rises Turnwise when viewed from the TOWER OF ART.

Grune

The summer gives garden or croft a languorous appeal. Such flowers that have been grown are now reaching their zenith. For the Cottage gardens are all ablaze in saffron and pink, and in the Town, Sweet Simperly will be oozing its pungent message across cobble and brick. But beware of Pocket Lice and Jerkunder, those nasty weeds that burrow and cling: the warm weather brings them out like a rash upon a tinker's elbow.

Herbs should be ready for distillation. Even the town garden can benefit from a Comfey Balm made from the common Comfey that forms in old drains and moist gutters. But we must warn against picking any from the environs of Unseen University: not only is it illegal (as all that is on thereon within without and withunder belongs to the University), it is also lethal. If you're caught collecting, you could end your days a frog; if you drink what you concoct, ditto.

'Tis now a time of storms on the great plains and a troubled time for those who travel the dusty roads. A moonstone or jade from the old empire will protect against lightning strike, though not against bandits or highwaymen. For that you must procure yourself a Stormwart, a rare gem that is found only on the graves of tailors: it will call down a thunderbolt on any highwaymen who approach.

Clean your ponds and ditches, so that the water will run pure, as all livestock may well feel the want of it ere long.

Midsummer is here, with Feasting, Merrymaking & sundry delights, and one or two rather more than just sundry.

A Midsummer Maid

1	OCTEDAY	
2	MONDAY	
3	TUESDAY	
4	WEDNESDAY	
5	THURSDAY	
6	FRIDAY	☾
7	SATURDAY	
8	SUNDAY	
9	OCTEDAY	
10	MONDAY	
11	TUESDAY	
12	WEDNESDAY	
13	THURSDAY	
14	FRIDAY	
15	SATURDAY	
16	SUNDAY	
17	OCTEDAY	
18	MONDAY	
19	TUESDAY	
20	WEDNESDAY	
21	THURSDAY	
22	FRIDAY	
23	SATURDAY	
24	SUNDAY	
25	OCTEDAY	
26	MONDAY	
27	TUESDAY	●
28	WEDNESDAY	
29	THURSDAY	
30	FRIDAY	
31	SATURDAY	
32	SUNDAY	

✷ AUGUST ✷

Of the Common Year.

Being the Number Unmentionable, but for this year most propitious as Melok doth rise into the house Melok. And this being a verdant time of the year on the Dysc, gives great benefit to all things that grow in the earth.

The Occasional Paddles do rise also into this house, but it is the men of sand who will benefit with a rain so strong and hard that their humped beasts of burden will wallow and cavort in much water. In Klatchistan, men will plot and a strange thing will be seen, and seen again by more people the following day. In NoThingFjord the address of the god Io and a small drawing of a hammer will be found written in seeds inside a pomegranate.

The month doth end with the Mystic house of the Star arriving hand in hand with the stars known to the ancients as Blik-Blick. She of the raven locks and voluptuous figure who serves at the temple, the high Priestess of Lu-Lu, is aknowing of all this but she says nought, save to blind shepherds or young men bearing gifts, and then, not a lot.

MAKERS OF FURNITURE AND THOSE WHO ENGINEER STAYS AND OTHER INTIMATE GARMENTS ARE WELL STARRED, AND WILL ENJOY MANY BENEFITS THIS MONTH, BUT MUST BE WARY OF SHELLFISH.

[32]

August

Seeds of all sorts can now be gathered, for whether in cot or town most every plant will be ripening. It was the old custom to share any spare seeds with neighbours. Indeed it is a custom we strongly recommend, but do be careful to give only seeds that you know will grow true. Many a feud has begun with some luckless soul planting a row of beans, to find next morning a row of huge stalks rising into the sky, taking up the whole garden, wrecking the foundations of the house, and blocking the door to the privy. This is of no use at all when the gardener merely wanted a few runners.

Harvesting now takes place and with it the traditional merrymakings that accompany this festive time, with platters of food, ale in huge quantities and cider by the jar. All are required before the harvest can be gathered. The prudent farmer will also employ the services of any Igor that can be obtained, as drunken reapers not only stack stooks of wheat and barley, but also feet, legs, and hands. Failing the use of an Igor, a bucket of boiling pitch and a sharp sacking needle and baling twine will do at a pinch.

Sewing wild oats: we are indeed the worse for the dwindling of this ancient tradition, and few indeed are the seamstresses deft enough to sew a bushel of long-bearded wild oats into a serviceable pair of shorts. In times past these were worn by those troubled by improper and vexatious thoughts, and we understand that there was nothing like a pair of wild-oat underthings, sewn hairy side in, to keep the mind very firmly on higher things.

Rummage your peas that have been left to dry, and more than once if the need be there, as not to do so will have them go green in the barn after a month or more. Treat cows against Luxation of the Treads with purple gargle.

In brewing for harvest, and in harvest, make three sorts of beer. The first Wort or strongest you may put by for your own use; the second, called best beer, whereof each man ought to have a pint in the morning before work starts, and as much at night as soon as he comes in. If work be carried on during the moon-shine, their share must be more. Small beer they must have in plenty at all times. Of Cider, give naught to the young, for it maketh them giggle.

| **Time and again wait for no man.** | Old Proverb |

1	OCTEDAY	
2	MONDAY	
3	TUESDAY	
4	WEDNESDAY	
5	THURSDAY	
6	FRIDAY	
7	SATURDAY	☽
8	SUNDAY	
9	OCTEDAY	
10	MONDAY	
11	TUESDAY	
12	WEDNESDAY	
13	THURSDAY	
14	FRIDAY	
15	SATURDAY	
16	SUNDAY	
17	OCTEDAY	
18	MONDAY	
19	TUESDAY	
20	WEDNESDAY	
21	THURSDAY	●
22	FRIDAY	
23	SATURDAY	
24	SUNDAY	
25	OCTEDAY	
26	MONDAY	
27	TUESDAY	
28	WEDNESDAY	
29	THURSDAY	
30	FRIDAY	
31	SATURDAY	
32	SUNDAY	

✴ SPUNE ✴

Of the Common Year.

Being the Ninth month, and one full of Mystic & Cosmic potential, some most untoward.

The House of The Star remains throughout, and entertains the Bright Cabbage early in the month. This Year the Starfish arrives mid-month which is the cause of much potency as House and Star do collude to do mischief. Be thankful then that the Old Dog calls at the end of the Month, giving a settling influence to all.

Wear a talisman of the Gate to ward off sharks, and do not step on any snake, even if invited.

A rain of tortoises, which could occasion a broken pate or two, will beset those in Skund but there is good eating on them, so all is equal. For the heavens both give and take away; just as once noblemen would keep a small charcoal brazier in their carriage, to heat pennies to red heat before tossing them to the beggars running alongside, so upon the starving the gods will rain heavy meatballs.

Spune

Fruit now hangs upon the bough in the orchard and soon will be ready for picking. Check your scumble press, and make sure you have put by such additives that give taste and body to this wondrous liquor, such as saltpetre, flowers of sulphur, old brass buttons and rats. If rats are not plentiful, a word to any gnome will result in a brace of the best ready to dunk. Be sure, also, that the pipes and runnels of the press be made of best lead, which doth add a wonderful sweetness to the brew. In the words of Friar Boy Odious, renowned Master of the Scumble: 'Fw'yo huzzy bwoy willeps hut? H'shush say wint!' Wise words indeed, and it would be a better world if they were followed by the feckless.

Soft fruits are a-plenty and the industrious husbandwomen will now be pickling, salting, drying, bottling, chutneying, stamping on and fermenting. Guard well your pickled onions, for they will be a magnet for all acquaintances who suddenly feel in need of charity, and may even arrive with a string bag. A sovereign remedy that will ensure you henceforward enjoy your pickles unmolested is the adding of a few chillis to some of the jars. Nevertheless, experience shows that by and large it is best to overproduce and give a little of the seedy, sloppy or unset jam to any neighbour, and two jars of each of the best to your local witch, especially if you wish to know on what side your bread is buttered. Jam is soon gone, but being a frog is for life.

The town garden can dry such herbs that have survived, and perhaps invest in a pig to fatten for Hogswatch.

Moles will be troublesome at this time, having been driven off the field by harvesting activities, and it is a fortunate husbandman who can acquire the services of one of the increasingly rare 'mole shouters'. He will turn up, with luck, wearing his moleskin trousers and hat decorated with mole skulls, and it is well worth watching his special mole dance as he works himself up into a rage against all moles. Then he will place his brightly coloured 'screaming tube' over the nearest molehill and shout down it so loudly that echoes will be heard underground. If sufficiently maddened, the mole shouter will chew himself down into the runs with his bare teeth, pull out the moles by hand and harangue them face to face. Part of the magic is in the words that are used, which are in no known language, and which have on occasion killed grass growing near the molehills.

1	OCTEDAY	
2	MONDAY	
3	TUESDAY	☾
4	WEDNESDAY	
5	THURSDAY	
6	FRIDAY	
7	SATURDAY	
8	SUNDAY	
9	OCTEDAY	
10	MONDAY	
11	TUESDAY	
12	WEDNESDAY	
13	THURSDAY	
14	FRIDAY	
15	SATURDAY	
16	SUNDAY	
17	OCTEDAY	
18	MONDAY	
19	TUESDAY	
20	WEDNESDAY	
21	THURSDAY	
22	FRIDAY	
23	SATURDAY	
24	SUNDAY	●
25	OCTEDAY	
26	MONDAY	
27	TUESDAY	
28	WEDNESDAY	
29	THURSDAY	
30	FRIDAY	
31	SATURDAY	
32	SUNDAY	

✳ SEKTOBER ✳

Of the Common Year.

Being the Tenth Month. The house of the Star is passing by, and in its last days is entered by Crabbus, its low light in the early autumn giving a message to those of Djeli with blue fingers. And then The Dog leaves us with good omens.

There cometh in this month great Ancient Ceremonies, powerful and tied to season for both Man & Dwarf alike. Their origins are like the taproot of the fig, hard to find except with gloves. But the wise of Krull, who know much of star gazing, say that a great calamity was averted, and the stars wheeled in the sky, and huge fires were lit, and those of magic were so scared that they stayed abed that night.

So be wary, for seven days after the New Moon, there begins what some will know as the Soul Cake Days. Celebrated by Dwarfs & Men with great fires, much noise, and mysterious customs, too many to catalogue, and some too moist to recommend.

Suffice to say, many children will be conceived those three nights of fevered firelight, and it's a wise child that knows its own father if its naming day is in June.

soul cake days

Sektober

Start sowing beans and barley if you are of a mind to do so, and it's a good idea to check your hives and make sure they are sheltered from the wind. This is also the time of salting meat, vegetables, and the elderly.

If you keep hogs, ring them now. The mellow tunes played on the autumn hog are a lovely sound in the mists of this season, especially if you have hogs of all sizes. Sadly, the days of the travelling bands of hog-ringers, who would play the whole of 'The Bells Of St Ungulant's' in seven parts for no more than half a pint of small beer, have long gone.

This month is when the eels will make their migration to the Circle Sea and they suddenly appear in the most unlikely places. There's good eating on a fat eel, and they smoke well, which makes them easier to catch as they often get out of breath on steep inclines.

The Soul Cake Days mark the start of the duck-hunting season, and apprentices and scholars will quit their places for a day out on the local ponds. This is a boon to the glass eye maker, as so many of our young men are abroad with bow and arrow and an enthusiasm for the chase that overrides their competence with this lethal weapon.

Even a man with one leg needs shoes.   Old Proverb

1	OCTEDAY	
2	MONDAY	
3	TUESDAY	
4	WEDNESDAY	
5	THURSDAY	
6	FRIDAY	
7	SATURDAY	
8	SUNDAY	
9	OCTEDAY	
10	MONDAY	☽
11	TUESDAY	
12	WEDNESDAY	
13	THURSDAY	
14	FRIDAY	
15	SATURDAY	
16	SUNDAY	
17	OCTEDAY	
18	MONDAY	
19	TUESDAY	
20	WEDNESDAY	
21	THURSDAY	
22	FRIDAY	
23	SATURDAY	
24	SUNDAY	●
25	OCTEDAY	
26	MONDAY	
27	TUESDAY	
28	WEDNESDAY	
29	THURSDAY	
30	FRIDAY	
31	SATURDAY	
32	SUNDAY	

✷ EMBER ✷

Of the Common Year.
Being the Eleventh Month.

This month is one of great import, for the firmament doth teem with stars beneficial to man and beast. The House of the Plough doth reside throughout, but within its sphere comes first The Flying Moose. A most potent sign for those who hunt.

A piece of Chalcony is a good talisman to have, and likewise Moonstone bound in silver. Also Beryl is a useful charm, for it staunches bleeding and stops puncture wounds from festering.

The Pitcher comes in to the House by the mid-month. This is good, though for this Common Year it will bring rain on the Ramtops. The Month exits with the coming of the Plough Handle, and that in the House of the Plough is mighty potent to those who live by the sod.

A newt called Nigel shall emerge from a river in far off NoThingFjord, and shall argue with all within hearing, in blank verse. And it will get mighty cross and stroppy, until at last it bursts into flame out of sheer indignation, and the people will wonder.

Howandaland shall have a mighty wave across its shore, followed by many dazed fish. Great will be the marine bounty, but few will survive to fry it.

Ember

This month is known by some folk in rural communities as 'the preacher' as it can be a little dull and rather wet.

It is a time for the wise husbandman to consider the lifting of the potatoes, the turning of the manure heap, and the cleaning of the drains, and so he will retire to his shed to consider this in full depth and maybe do a little light re-arranging of his jars of nails and screws.

Nuts abound; even in the great city going a-nutting is a favoured pastime of Ember amongst the young men. In the lanes, drovers' ways and foot-paths, the beech, walnut, pine and gripe are heavy with their armoured progeny, but be wary, as an unripe gripenut has been known to explode with enough force to blow off a hand.

Fungi also are now appearing under trees, hedgerows and armpits. Here our town dwellers have equal picking to those in the country, as many varieties of interesting fungi can be found in damp and oozing places. Many are the books with colour plates that profess to tell the city dweller which fungi can be safely eaten and great is his or her puzzlement when he or she peruseth the beguiling pages, for it would seem that the Gnat's Deathcap can be told from the Horse Truffle only by close exam-ination of the gollets, which turn purple if pressed with a silver spoon, as well they might. And so the cautious reader sighs and has beans on toast again. But it is ever our desire to inform and enlighten, and we can therefore assure our readers, whom we wish to preserve, that there are only two facts to bear in mind when selecting fungi:

1. ALL FUNGI ARE EDIBLE.

2. SOME FUNGI ARE NOT EDIBLE MORE THAN ONCE.

1	OCTEDAY	
2	MONDAY	
3	TUESDAY	
4	WEDNESDAY	
5	THURSDAY	
6	FRIDAY	
7	SATURDAY	
8	SUNDAY	
9	OCTEDAY	
10	MONDAY	
11	TUESDAY	☾
12	WEDNESDAY	
13	THURSDAY	
14	FRIDAY	
15	SATURDAY	
16	SUNDAY	
17	OCTEDAY	
18	MONDAY	
19	TUESDAY	
20	WEDNESDAY	
21	THURSDAY	
22	FRIDAY	
23	SATURDAY	
24	SUNDAY	
25	OCTEDAY	
26	MONDAY	
27	TUESDAY	●
28	WEDNESDAY	
29	THURSDAY	
30	FRIDAY	
31	SATURDAY	
32	SUNDAY	

✶ DECEMBER ✶

Of the Common Year,
Being the Twelfth Month.
In the House of the Plough do we stay for but three more weeks, till that bringer of folly doth wander in as a pedlar or mountebank.

Okjock the Salesman is a-calling and bringing his wares, some handsome, some tawdry, some that thou knowst not the what of, until too late. But he lights up the lives of beggars, and those who wander the land selling to magistrate and dairymaid alike. He swives the both in his way, the one gets a ribbon for her pleasure, the other a robbin', 'tis the old saying.

Those who dwell in towns are starred this time, for they live by their wits & commerce. For them we say, beware gold, cherish silver and mind the copper, for it doth add up to all. There is no working charm against Okjock, he has them all aplenty and will sell you a pocketful ere he is done. However, a pewter representation of a foot in a door is sometimes efficacious, if heavy enough.

THOSE WHO WANDER THE HUBLAND STEPPES ARE IN FOR A MIGHTY SHOCK, FOR THE STARS FORETELL A MIGHTY STORM, WHICH SHALL CAUSE THE EARTH TO TREMBLE A DAY AND A NIGHT, BEFORE THE WATER ABATES. THEN THERE SHALL BE A PLAGUE OF GREAT LIZARDS, FEARSOME TO BEHOLD, THAT WILL VOMIT FORTH FIRE. 'TIS BEST NOT TO GO THERE THAT WEEK.

In the mighty Ramtops a sign will be given that shall be totally ignored, which is as usual for those parts, where there are signs all the time.

December

The celebration of Hogswatch dominates the month but there are still chores to be done for the husbandman liveth, as it were, with one foot in tomorrow. In the garden dig a square hole and in it put your cabbage stumps; cover them first with earth, and then with straw, and then with earth. By this way you shall have early greens, it is said, although the good husbandman will remark that an early crop of slugs is more likely. Set garlic and beans for an early start next year.

Bend your mind to your compost heaps, turning them in good time to prevent a sudden exhalation of noxious vapours. If a critical mass is reached, the resultant explosion can cover a wide area with great expectorations. The muck should be spread on your land, not the fields of your neighbour! Turn it gently and allow air in to breathe. Do not neglect soot, a sovereign aid for the soil. Get your chimneys swept, and use the soot, crisped sweep's boy, etc. to garnish, and cover with straw.

This month the soot carts will be rolling out from Ankh-Morpork and most towns and villages will have soot auctions. The prudent man will buy his soot well in advance from one of the many Soot Captains and beat the rush. How strange it is that those who dwell around that great metropolis look forward not to its fashions, its dances, or its fads but the soot carts, the horse-dung barges and the night soil wagons, which will make the fields bloom again. The city's wastes are the countryman's treasure. When the good husbandman ponders on this he will feel in awe of the beneficent workings of Providence, or else get good and mad.

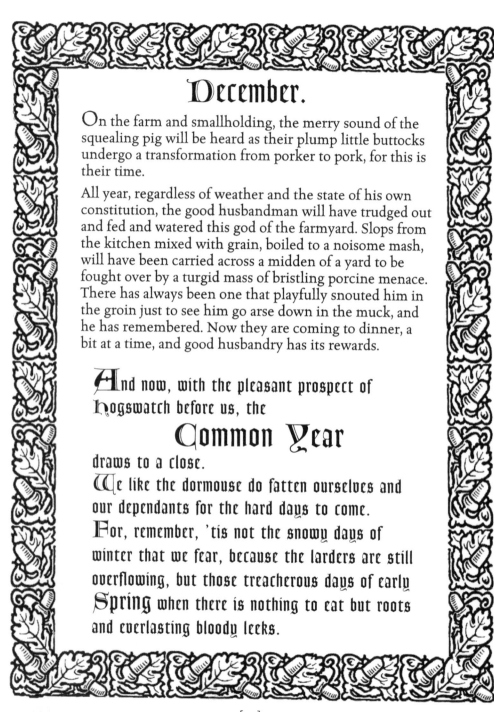

December.

On the farm and smallholding, the merry sound of the squealing pig will be heard as their plump little buttocks undergo a transformation from porker to pork, for this is their time.

All year, regardless of weather and the state of his own constitution, the good husbandman will have trudged out and fed and watered this god of the farmyard. Slops from the kitchen mixed with grain, boiled to a noisome mash, will have been carried across a midden of a yard to be fought over by a turgid mass of bristling porcine menace. There has always been one that playfully snouted him in the groin just to see him go arse down in the muck, and he has remembered. Now they are coming to dinner, a bit at a time, and good husbandry has its rewards.

And now, with the pleasant prospect of hogswatch before us, the

Common Year

draws to a close.

We like the dormouse do fatten ourselves and our dependants for the hard days to come.

For, remember, 'tis not the snowy days of winter that we fear, because the larders are still overflowing, but those treacherous days of early Spring when there is nothing to eat but roots and everlasting bloody leeks.

Alas, we seldom these days see a real pig borer, but in times past almost every village had one as a kindly alternative to the butcher's knife. He or she would of course work alone, because it was dangerous for another human to get within earshot when they were telling the stories, and even so the occasional fowl or overflying bird would succumb. A favoured theme was anecdotes about the legal and judicial aspects of cheese, and every borer had his – or her, in many cases – prized and jealously guarded collection of suicidally dull tales. It is more than thirty years since the last Pig Boring Championship, when Mistress Edith Leakall's pig passed away peacefully only nine minutes into her story about her friend Mrs Insufflator's problems with her knee.

But these days we must be all at a rush and there is no time for such skill, and so people resort to the knife, which is quicker but noisier and certainly messier.

For those of you who have kept a porker in the town garden, we do not recommend you do this yourself. Neighbours can get the wrong impression, and the Watch, even if they believe you, will take the pig in as evidence. Far better to take it to a butcher and share the proceeds, but be wary: if all you get back is six trotters and a bag of bones, then you have either been fiddled or it was a very odd pig.

Those Ancients of Krull who gazed long into the heavens and mapped the firmament, those wise men who watched the watchers from the high Tower of Art, and so did cunningly avail themselves of those secrets, and even those ancient men who sat in front of their caves and said 'There! Doesn't that sort of look like a parsnip made of stars to you, if you half-close one eye?'...all have contributed to the knowledge we presently share with you.

For now we lay down our astrolabes, telescopes, and calculus, and earn our day of rest before once again searching the sky for the footprint of the stars, that your profit and pleasure may be afforded.

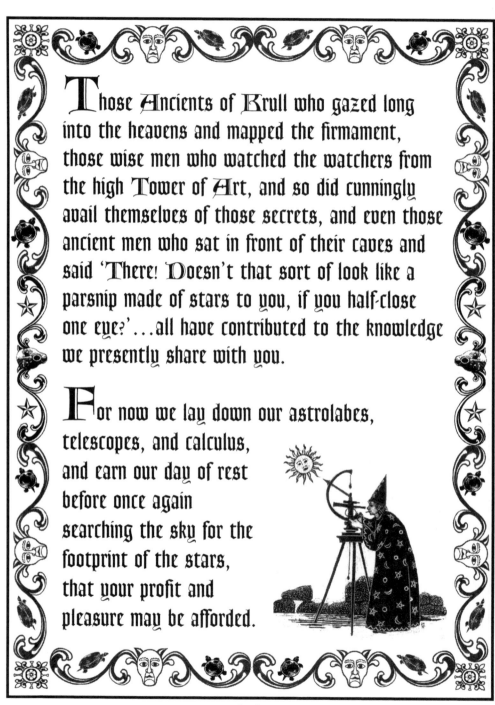

Our Astrological Heritage

Of the two great centres of Astrological Learning, Ankh-Morpork is the oldest, although there is a paucity of evidence of this save the remains of devices within the Tower of Art and some charts and notations in the Library, including one on which has been scrawled, apparently several thousand years ago, a notation that translates as: 'I think we could make a bob or two out of this'.

Astronomy, which is the bedrock of Astrology in the same way that the skeletal structure of the body supports the intellect of the brain, has been of some interest to the denizens of Unseen University, and they have a perfectly workable observation platform. But this is considerably lower than the Tower of Art, and is remarkable only for its revolving armchair with attached ashtray, which dispenses with the necessity for strenuous movement.

Certainly there is no Professor of Astrology in the University and, until recently, it was held in almost universal contempt by the faculty. After all, it was just about things moving around. If you waited long enough, they came around again. This did not strike the wizards as particularly interesting.

Krull, however, has had a thriving Astrological tradition for many centuries, as the study of the stars was pertinent to their indigenous religion. Indeed the head of the religious order and laity was, and is, The Arch Astronomer. When you live on the edge of the world and can see from night into day just by craning a little, the universe tends to prey on your mind more than somewhat. The Krullians have never fallen victim to the perennial heresy that the world is globular and it makes no kind of sense, because they've even mapped large parts of the Turtle's head. When you've measured the albedo of an eye thirty miles across, it's hard to be persuaded that it doesn't exist.

And thus the Geography of the Dysc and the location of the respective observatories influenced the direction and content of their respective disciplines.

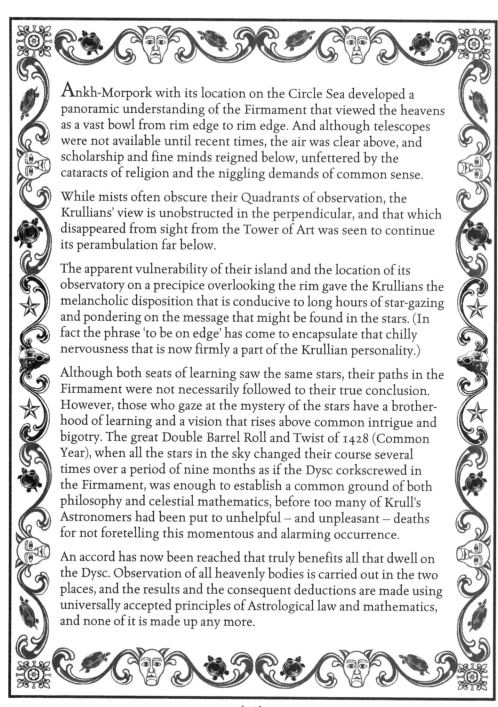

Ankh-Morpork with its location on the Circle Sea developed a panoramic understanding of the Firmament that viewed the heavens as a vast bowl from rim edge to rim edge. And although telescopes were not available until recent times, the air was clear above, and scholarship and fine minds reigned below, unfettered by the cataracts of religion and the niggling demands of common sense.

While mists often obscure their Quadrants of observation, the Krullians' view is unobstructed in the perpendicular, and that which disappeared from sight from the Tower of Art was seen to continue its perambulation far below.

The apparent vulnerability of their island and the location of its observatory on a precipice overlooking the rim gave the Krullians the melancholic disposition that is conducive to long hours of star-gazing and pondering on the message that might be found in the stars. (In fact the phrase 'to be on edge' has come to encapsulate that chilly nervousness that is now firmly a part of the Krullian personality.)

Although both seats of learning saw the same stars, their paths in the Firmament were not necessarily followed to their true conclusion. However, those who gaze at the mystery of the stars have a brother-hood of learning and a vision that rises above common intrigue and bigotry. The great Double Barrel Roll and Twist of 1428 (Common Year), when all the stars in the sky changed their course several times over a period of nine months as if the Dysc corkscrewed in the Firmament, was enough to establish a common ground of both philosophy and celestial mathematics, before too many of Krull's Astronomers had been put to unhelpful – and unpleasant – deaths for not foretelling this momentous and alarming occurrence.

An accord has now been reached that truly benefits all that dwell on the Dysc. Observation of all heavenly bodies is carried out in the two places, and the results and the consequent deductions are made using universally accepted principles of Astrological law and mathematics, and none of it is made up any more.

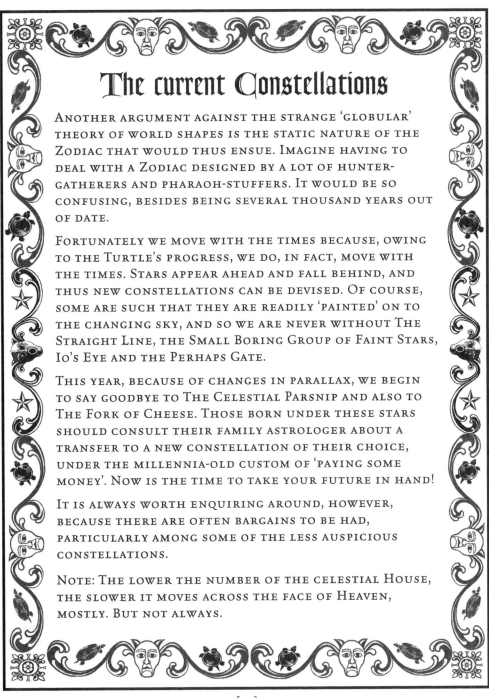

The current Constellations

ANOTHER ARGUMENT AGAINST THE STRANGE 'GLOBULAR' THEORY OF WORLD SHAPES IS THE STATIC NATURE OF THE ZODIAC THAT WOULD THUS ENSUE. IMAGINE HAVING TO DEAL WITH A ZODIAC DESIGNED BY A LOT OF HUNTER-GATHERERS AND PHARAOH-STUFFERS. IT WOULD BE SO CONFUSING, BESIDES BEING SEVERAL THOUSAND YEARS OUT OF DATE.

FORTUNATELY WE MOVE WITH THE TIMES BECAUSE, OWING TO THE TURTLE'S PROGRESS, WE DO, IN FACT, MOVE WITH THE TIMES. STARS APPEAR AHEAD AND FALL BEHIND, AND THUS NEW CONSTELLATIONS CAN BE DEVISED. OF COURSE, SOME ARE SUCH THAT THEY ARE READILY 'PAINTED' ON TO THE CHANGING SKY, AND SO WE ARE NEVER WITHOUT THE STRAIGHT LINE, THE SMALL BORING GROUP OF FAINT STARS, IO'S EYE AND THE PERHAPS GATE.

THIS YEAR, BECAUSE OF CHANGES IN PARALLAX, WE BEGIN TO SAY GOODBYE TO THE CELESTIAL PARSNIP AND ALSO TO THE FORK OF CHEESE. THOSE BORN UNDER THESE STARS SHOULD CONSULT THEIR FAMILY ASTROLOGER ABOUT A TRANSFER TO A NEW CONSTELLATION OF THEIR CHOICE, UNDER THE MILLENNIA-OLD CUSTOM OF 'PAYING SOME MONEY'. NOW IS THE TIME TO TAKE YOUR FUTURE IN HAND!

IT IS ALWAYS WORTH ENQUIRING AROUND, HOWEVER, BECAUSE THERE ARE OFTEN BARGAINS TO BE HAD, PARTICULARLY AMONG SOME OF THE LESS AUSPICIOUS CONSTELLATIONS.

NOTE: THE LOWER THE NUMBER OF THE CELESTIAL HOUSE, THE SLOWER IT MOVES ACROSS THE FACE OF HEAVEN, MOSTLY. BUT NOT ALWAYS.

The Zodiac. Star list

The First House
THE HOUSE OF IO

1 THE EYE OF IO
2 THE CRAB
3 THE COW OF HEAVEN
4 THE STRING
ALSO KNOWN AS
THE KNOTTED STRING
5 THE CELESTIAL PARSNIP

The Second House
THE HOUSE OF THE GATE

6 WEZEN
KNOWN ALSO AS WEZEN THE
TWO-HEADED KANGAROO
7 TWO FAT COUSINS
8 THE PERHAPS GATE
9 SCARAB'S CLAW
10 MUBBO THE HYENA

The Third House
THE HOUSE OF THE BULL

11 SILICAROUS'S GIFT
12 THE BULL
13 HAST'S TRUMPET
14 CUBAL'S FLAME
15 THE VOID

The Fourth House
THE HOUSE OF MELOK

16 MELOK
17 OLD TOESY
18 VUT THE EVENSTAR
19 MR WILLIAMS
20 OCCASIONAL PADDLES

The Fifth House
THE HOUSE OF THE BRIGHT CABBAGE

21 BLIK-BLICK
22 THE BRIGHT CABBAGE
23 THE STARFISH
24 OLD DOG
25 CRABBUS

The Sixth House
THE HOUSE OF THE PLOUGH

26 PASHMINA
27 THE FLYING MOOSE
28 THE PITCHER
OR SOME WOULD SAY BUCKET
29 PLOUGH HANDLE
30 OKJOCK THE SALESMAN

The Seventh House
THE HOUSE OF THE STAR

31 THE FAINT STAR MAJOR
32 THE FAINT STAR MINOR
33 THE LITTLE TURTLE
34 THE FLAGON
35 KET'S KNIFE

The Seven and One
THE HOUSE OF WOLDAR

36 WOLDAR
37 EVAR'S FOOTPRINT
38 THE RAM'S HORN
39 TWO RIVERS
40 YOUNG FAITHFUL

The Ninth House
THE HOUSE OF THE RAM

41 THE JUMPING RAM
42 KHEFIN'S EYE 1
43 KHEFIN'S EYE 2
44 KHEFIN'S EYE 3
45 KHEFIN'S EYE 4

The Tenth House
THE HOUSE OF TRABNOR

46 TRABNOR
47 THE LANTHORN
48 THE WICKET
49 TURNIP'S TAIL
50 THE SNIPE

The Eleventh House
THE HOUSE OF THE HORSE

51 TEG THE HORSE
52 THE MILLER'S POCKET
53 ASTORIA'S FLAME
54 THE CRADLE
55 THE SLEEPING DOG

The Twelfth House
THE HOUSE OF FORE AND AFT

56 YOUNG HARRY
57 FORWARD
58 AFT
59 VUT'S CANDLE
60 SILUR THE CATFISH

The Thirteenth House
THE DREAD HOUSE

61 OLD FAITHFUL
62 THE SCYTHE
63 THE COFFEE CUP
64 GAHOOLIE THE VASE OF TULIPS

The First House

1 THE EYE OF IO
Of the First House.
A singular Brightness of a single star, that shines regardless of the Moon's vigour. Of use in the spells of love truth, and nocturnal investigation. The first sign of the first House; all great Kings and Potentates are said to be born under or blessed by this star, because of the accuracy needed to get born under it.

2 THE CRAB
Of the First House.
Three stars in formation sideways moving across the heavens.
Under this sign look for water magic and treasure buried betwixt earth and sea. Some do say that those born under this sign are avaricious and, if a woman, inclined to store peas.

3 THE COW OF HEAVEN
Of the First House.
Five stars in form of a cow with full udders.
This is a sign of plenty in man and beast. Much used as a charm for milkmaids and those young women who yearn for a career in the field of entertainment.

4 THE STRING
Also known as THE KNOTTED STRING
Of the First House.
A myriad of small stars that seem to slowly twist.
Capital in the evocation for spells to aid the birthing of livestock and women and lawyers. It is written that those born under this star are cloven minded and sometimes word shy.

5 THE CELESTIAL PARSNIP
Of the First House.
One vast star with a tail of 3 stars preceded by weaker celestial brethren of a greenish hue. Its appearance in the night sky is a sure sign of severe frost, that which will kill the lesser but cause its Dyscworld namesake to flourish and flavour. Hated by some and loved by others for that very reason. Otherwise not as magical as it is thought, though some say those born under this star are good with root vegetables of all varieties, if that is considered to be a talent. The Parsnip will become unrecognizable by Ember.

The Second House

6 WEZEN
Known also as WEZEN THE TWO-HEADED KANGAROO
Of the Second House.
Seen as up to 13 stars, the very outline of which is suggestive of this
Foureckian beast. Under this sign are drunkards conceived, but it is
favoured by prisoners who regard it as a good omen if seen when going
'over the wall'.

7 TWO FAT COUSINS
Of the Second House.
Being 2 large and bright stars that move in ponderous formation across
the sky like a fat man on his way to a third helping. Under this sign are
pastry cooks often conceived, and in its light the finest lard will be turned
to gold, it is said. Experimental astrologers have found this is not the case.

8 THE PERHAPS GATE
Of the Second House.
At least 8 stars in an open square, or not.
Those who are lost or face troubles of the heart can find solace in its
contemplation, or not.

9 SCARAB'S CLAW
Of the Second House.
Three stars around a third giving a strange bright light. When spells are
set within its house and light they are indeed most potent. Also evoked
by dentists. No one knows why.

10 MUBBO THE HYENA
Of the Second House.
This small group of stars seem to chase behind the Cow of Heaven, hence
their name. As they never seem to catch her, they are regarded as the sign
of the prowler or tax gatherer. Not a good sign to be born under.

The Third House

11 SILICAROUS'S GIFT
Of the Third House.
The stars that form a triangle with a tail.
Noted by many as being a bringer of gentle breezes and spring weather.
Also rains of fish. Liked by many landlocked communities, where fish are
otherwise expensive.

12 THE BULL
Of the Third House.
A large star & Rampant with what appear to be horns.
Known to be most useful in matters of husbandry that require a fruitful
outcome. Much used as a talisman by bridegrooms.
Some do say that those born of this sign are like unto a bull themselves in
temperament and temper.

13 HAST'S TRUMPET
Of the Third House.
Three small stars quite dim and one being most bright, in the shape of an
instrument for lifting beets. A foreteller of doom in men, but plenty in
camels. Used in conjunction with the charming of snakes.

14 CUBAL'S FLAME
Of the Third House.
One star in fiery temperament that flies by red in hue.
When seen rising over Rim or Mountain rampant fire will surely follow.
Capital as an evocation to ease heartburn and fever. Those with red hair or
fiery temperament are said to be conceived under this star's influence.

15 THE VOID
Of the Third House.
Not easy to see unless the weather be exceptionally clear. To the
uninitiated, it is a patch of sky with no stars. People born under this
constellation are seldom seen and, indeed, may be invisible.

The Fourth House

16 MELOK
Of the Fourth House.
Two stars spinning, one brighter than its fellow.
Evoked by priests of Bast, it is said. No one knows why.

17 OLD TOESY
Of the Fourth House.
Nine large stars but dim and seeming flat about, as a cough sweet or button.
If quick, a spell cast under its light is most good for promoting the growth of fine Horseradish.

18 VUT THE EVENSTAR
Of the Fourth House.
One star always seen on the Rim from dusk.
Beloved by lovers, but hated by poets because it doesn't rhyme with anything very romantic except, perhaps, butt. Otherwise of no practical use.

19 MR WILLIAMS
Of the Fourth House.
Not a constellation as such, but apparently the body of Bosun Williams, who was washed off the deck of the clipper *Dancing Mary* off the coast of Fourecks and was blown so far off the Rim by the gale that he appears to have gone into orbit. It is believed that he will re-enter the atmosphere around February 5, and as a mark of respect readers are enjoined not to wish upon any falling stars that night.

20 OCCASIONAL PADDLES
Of the Fourth House.
A strange star seldom seen unless under the clearest desert sky. Sacred to scarab beetles. People who sell individual roses in restaurants are born under this star.

The Fifth House

21 BLIK-BLICK
Of the Fifth House.
Not much known save a fleeting glimpse one night by the high priestess
of Lu-Lu, who swears by it.

22 THE BRIGHT CABBAGE
Of the Fifth House.
A green-hued single star, currently low in the sky.
Not believed in by many learned sages, but evoked by bucolic hedge
wizards at harvest time in the Sto Plains. It is thought to aid the
fermentation of root beer, and ease – or possibly cause, the ancient texts
disagree – the flatulent stomach.

23 THE STARFISH
Of the Fifth House.
Twelve stars that wheel like chariot spokes.
Otherwise unremarkable and of no known use. Believed to exist because
of the embarrassment otherwise caused by blank spaces in the firmament.

24 OLD DOG
Of the Fifth House.
Two stars that are close, one being red, the other yellow.
Capital, it is said, for brewers' settling spells, and also gazed at by
nocturnal pipe smokers at sea. This is the star under which bait-diggers
are born.

25 CRABBUS
Of the Fifth House.
A single star almost blue, but sometimes greenish. A star of mediocre
omen. That is to say, events occasioned by it tend to be rather dull and
unnoticed, as are the people.

Being born in a stable doesn't make you a horse.   Old Proverb

The Sixth House

26 PASHMINA
Of the Sixth House.
A skein of small faint stars like a fine woollen scarf.
Said to enter the dreams of lovers, wherein it produces a sweet
contentment, which vanishes at cockcrow.

27 THE FLYING MOOSE
Of the Sixth House.
A most singular collection, just like its namesake. It looks just like a
moose.
Loved by hunters, who throw spears at it when drunk. Since this
constellation is currently overhead, it performs a useful service by
reducing the number of stupid hunters. Used by some in the making of
hangover cures.

28 THE PITCHER
Or some would say BUCKET
Of the Sixth House.
Three small stars in front of a number of others.
Nothing is known to their detriment.

29 PLOUGH HANDLE
Of the Sixth House.
The definite shape of a plough handle is formed by these stars.
Although they move at some speed across the night sky, it is said a good
ploughman and team of oxen can match their pace. Credulous people are
born under these stars.

30 OKJOCK THE SALESMAN
Of the Sixth House.
The brightest of this house.
This star seems to follow you everywhere in the night sky, and is seen
through windows, and even keyholes. Once seen, it is like dung on a
boot, almost impossible to shake off. Has been known to follow people
home and try to contact them at their place of work.

The Seventh House

31 THE FAINT STAR MAJOR
Of the Seventh House.
Very faint at times but sometimes brighter.

32 THE FAINT STAR MINOR
Of the Seventh House.
Very faint at all times.

We must admit that these are rather ordinary stars. There have been efforts made to smarten them up but, frankly, this area of sky has nothing much to recommend it. People born under these stars are advised to lie about it.

33 THE LITTLE TURTLE
Of the Seventh House.
Large but not too bright, being one star above two more, and then three. When viewed over still water, its reflection gives it its name, although you have to want to see the turtle, if you see what we mean. A useful constellation.

34 THE FLAGON
Of the Seventh House.
Not often seen except in the marshes near Tsort from where, it is said, its influence extends to crocodiles and bits of rock.

35 KET'S KNIFE
Of the Seventh House.
A strange star group in the shape of a spiral, much like an embalmer's brain-removing knife as used in Djelibeybi. Probably has great significance to embalmers and sommeliers. People born under this sign do not like garlic.

It's the spilt milk that sours the quickest.   Old Proverb

The Seven and One

36 WOLDAR
Of the Seven and 1st House.
Very big, but very dim.
Named after one of the old gods, who resembled it in many ways. It has
no power now, it is believed.

37 EVAR'S FOOTPRINT
Of the Seven and 1st House.
A pulsing star that moves across the quadrant.
Old tales tell of its use in conjuring images of past journeys.
Camel Drivers and Muleteers are born under this sign.

38 THE RAM'S HORN
Of the Seven and 1st House.
Like unto a ram's horn and thus looked for by shepherds. Shepherds and
herdsmen are said to be blessed if conceived under its light.

39 TWO RIVERS
Of the Seven and 1st House.
Small nebulous streams of faint stars, but blue at times.
Believed once to have been the necklace of some great Goddess. Her
name though has fallen into disuse, and all that was known about her is
lost. There may be no truth in it.

40 YOUNG FAITHFUL
Of the Seven and 1st House.
A blue to white star. Rather fast, but steady in the sky.
Much of late has been written concerning the attributes of this strange
celestial visitor. Nothing occult seems to occur, but that is no guarantee
that it might not. It is being watched, just in case. People born under this
star are slightly paranoid.

The Ninth House

41 THE JUMPING RAM
Of the Ninth House.
You could confuse this with the Ram's Horn.
Don't.

42 KHEFIN'S EYE 1
Of the Ninth House.

43 KHEFIN'S EYE 2
Of the Ninth House.

44 KHEFIN'S EYE 3
Of the Ninth House.

45 KHEFIN'S EYE 4
Of the Ninth House.
People born under this star are called Khefin or have very good eyesight
or know someone called Khefin who has.

All these stars are best seen in Djelibeybi where they are accorded much
reverence.

Even vultures sometimes throw up.

Old Ephebian Proverb

The Tenth House

46 TRABNOR
Of the Tenth House.
A mighty white bright star. Most useful to Soothsayers and Mystics as its
path and house act as a celestial signpost in the casting of runes.
A capital sign to be born under for Mystics & Horse Dealers.

47 THE LANTHORN
Of the Tenth House.
One bright star that moves as though carried. Those born under it will
find what they seek, except for keys.

48 THE WICKET
Of the Tenth House.
As an open gate or small portal through which other stars are seen.
Because of its speed it seems to have little use as an augury of good or ill.
Though 'tis said that if you wish upon it, having lost a key at night, the
door will open. But you have to be quick, for it will readily close again.

49 TURNIP'S TAIL
Of the Tenth House.
Small stars that some hold to resemble a Turnip, though not I, for I
suspect it to be but a celestial shadow of its Ponderous Cousin, the
Parsnip. If born under this star, lie.

50 THE SNIPE
Of the Tenth House.
This bright little star rises from behind The Perhaps Gate like a snipe
from the rushes. Spectacular when seen, but no other use.
Actors are born under this star.

A lame man can still count on his feet.

Old Proverb

The Eleventh House

51 TEG THE HORSE
Of the Eleventh House.
A magnificent group of stars, like unto a fine stallion with flowing mane.
Worshipped as a manifestation of the Djelibeybi God of Agriculture,
therefore sometimes used in conjunction with growing spells when the
weather is dry.
Any foal born under this sign is sure to be fleet of foot, and any man to
have a kinship with horses.

52 THE MILLER'S POCKET
Of the Eleventh House.
A black hole in the middle of a small group of feeble stars.
Useless to wish upon. Doleful and mean are said to be the attributes of
those born under this sign.

53 ASTORIA'S FLAME
Of the Eleventh House.
Very bright, but quick, and of a reddish yellow in hue. It is reported to be
beneficial for maidens to wish upon to see the name of their intended
cast from the shadow of a peeled apple. Mostly rural in its application, I
would venture.
A good sign to conceive under.

54 THE CRADLE
Of the Eleventh House.
This star does have the colour of a pink blush, and does follow on from
the previous.
It is said to bring a morning sickness to those maidens who are now not,
after messing about with apple cores and young men in orchards at night.

55 THE SLEEPING DOG
Of the Eleventh House.
Said to resemble a sleeping dog, though there is some dispute amongst
Sages and Lore Masters, who contend it could be a sleeping log.
Ancient writ is uncertain in this respect. Under this sign are born
veterinary surgeons, or possibly lumberjacks. Research is continuing.

The Twelfth House

56 YOUNG HARRY
Of the Twelfth House.
Again there is some confusion due to the speed of this star; it could also
be Young Hairy.

57 FORWARD
Of the Twelfth House.
This star, it has been determined, occupies that point in space to which
the Turtle is heading, although it is in fact not a star at all but a tiny point
of darkness against a wash of glowing gas. No doubt its nature will be
revealed in due course. Those born under this star are always looking
forward to tomorrow.

58 AFT
Of the Twelfth House.
A large red star, visited by the Turtle in recent astronomical history,
where we were fortunate to witness the birth of a number of new sky
turtles whose eggs had incubated in the warm glow as on a beach. Those
born under this star are beginning to make their mark as historians and
others of that sort who hanker after the past.

59 VUT'S CANDLE
Of the Twelfth House.
Bright and at times flickering to the eye.
One of the High Priests of Djelibeybi vouchsafed to me wondrous tales of
mystic magic wrought within its influence. However I was never quick
enough.

60 SILUR THE CATFISH
Of the Twelfth House.
Not much seen; nor, I believe, is anything influenced by this star. It may
not exist.

The Thirteenth House

61 OLD FAITHFUL
Of the Thirteenth House.
Rarely seen due to its speed. Nothing else is known of it, though it may be a cause of rains of bedsteads as it disturbs the aetheric substances.

62 THE SCYTHE
Of the Thirteenth House.
Most powerful a sign.
Can only be seen by Wizards. Do not ask any more. Best not to be born under this star. Parents should make their arrangements accordingly.

63 THE COFFEE CUP
Of the Thirteenth House.
A modern constellation, and unfortunately named by a young research astrologer with little appreciation of the beauty of language. It is in the shape of, all right, a coffee cup (but if constellations are going to be named purely on their shape, we would have far too many Random Groupings Of Stars). People born under this sign are nervous.

64 GAHOOLIE THE VASE OF TULIPS
Of the Thirteenth House.
All who try to hold this star in their gaze tend to suffer a great commotion of the brain. When senses return, if the beholder have any sanity left, all they can tell is that they saw what after a while appeared to be a huge vase of Tulips. Wise men and Sages say that this is but the dread remains of a vision so powerful the mind of man is not tempered to behold it. No spell is cast within its boundary, nor prophecy made upon its travail. That's proper astrology, that is.

Without the Scholarship and detailed observations of the Firmament by the Monks of Krull, and their rigorous mathematical extrapolation by Professor Truran, this portion of the Almanak could never have been written. It would have been easier for the layman to understand, but useless.

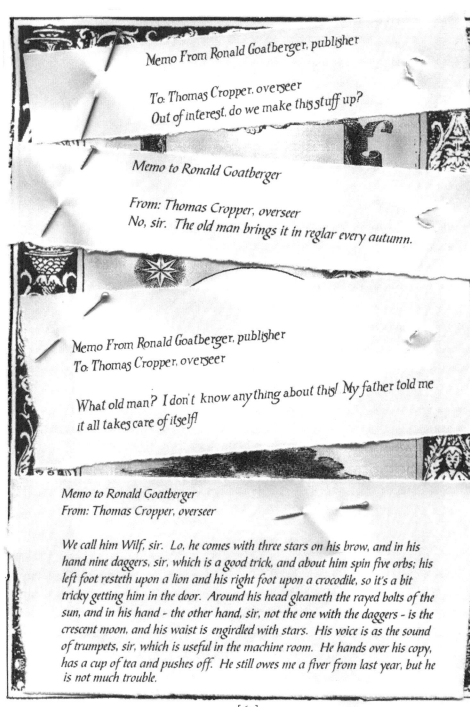

Memo From Ronald Goatberger, publisher

To: Thomas Cropper, overseer
Out of interest, do we make this stuff up?

Memo to Ronald Goatberger

From: Thomas Cropper, overseer
No, sir. The old man brings it in reglar every autumn.

Memo From Ronald Goatberger, publisher
To: Thomas Cropper, overseer

What old man? I don't know anything about this! My father told me it all takes care of itself!

Memo to Ronald Goatberger
From: Thomas Cropper, overseer

We call him Wilf, sir. Lo, he comes with three stars on his brow, and in his hand nine daggers, sir, which is a good trick, and about him spin five orbs; his left foot resteth upon a lion and his right foot upon a crocodile, so it's a bit tricky getting him in the door. Around his head gleameth the rayed bolts of the sun, and in his hand - the other hand, sir, not the one with the daggers - is the crescent moon, and his waist is engirdled with stars. His voice is as the sound of trumpets, sir, which is useful in the machine room. He hands over his copy, has a cup of tea and pushes off. He still owes me a fiver from last year, but he is not much trouble.

The Hierarchy of the Stars

The house predominant is like the father, ruling either with a soft or harsh hand depending on mood and occasion.

Each Star entering or leaving a house is Subservient, or Aggressive, depending on aspect and whim.

Rising is Aggressive, and called Martial.

Regressing, or passing from the threshold, is of the gentler persuasion, and becomes Distaff.

Memo From Ronald Goatberger, publisher
To: Thomas Cropper, overseer

That sounds unbelievable, Mr Cropper!

Memo to Ronald Goatberger

From: Thomas Cropper, overseer

Ah, sir, this is Ankh-Morpork. Most people wouldn't bother to turn their heads when he walks down the street, except he moves a bit tricky, what with the lion walking faster than the crocodile which, actually, Zeb the apprentice says, is really an alligator. Young Zeb reckons Wilf is the God of the Celestial Orbs and Geometries, 'cos he looks like a picture in the frontispiece of an old book he's seen. As you might imagine, I was a bit worried about this, but Zeb said he's not a major god any more since stuff pretty much happens by itself these days. But astrologers and such believe in him, so he's hanging on, you might say.

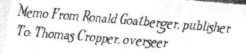

Memo From Ronald Goatberger, publisher
To: Thomas Cropper, overseer

Mr Cropper, do you really mean to suggest that our astrological predictions are actually written by the deity in charge? That's unbelievable!

Memo to Ronald Goatberger
From: Thomas Cropper, overseer

Seems sensible to me, sir. At least he knows what's going on, but he says he keeps it a bit vague 'cos of quantum. Our milkman has a part-time job as the fifth Horseman of the Apocalypse, but you'd never know it from his yoghurt. You get used to this around here. Anyway, I think the old boy can use the money, 'cos I don't imagine celestial orbs pay well.

Io is in Prime until day 63 of Offle (Scholar's Year). Then The Gate is rising, both being Martial until Grune.

Io in Offle to 54/2/SY Martial till 18/2/SY. The Crab enters opposite Scarab's Claw which will rise on 37/2/SY. Thus any born under that sign will have a predilection for yellow hair and hammer toes, but will sing in tune.

Their favourite colour will be blue.

The Cow of Heaven enters Io on the 27/1/SY and leaves through the Gate in February, but occludes in part The String on the 38th and The Parsnip on the 51st. These stars balance the Martial and the Distaff without detriment to any. The Wezen is Distaff but The Scarab's Claw is Martial and opposite. Thus when it arrives on the 37/2/SY those born between Muntab and Hersheba on the 20/2/SY will have a surprise in store.

The Perhaps Gate comes into the House of its name on the 25th, and this is auspicious for those seeking entry. Any born on that date will unfortunately be unable to make up their minds.

Mubbo circles the fold but in the Distaff, and Silicarous's Gift is low on the rim and in the Distaff as a new house is awaiting.

The house of the Bull in ascendance with the Star of The Bull Entering from the 3rd Quadrant of Krull. Begins the Month of March in the Scholastic Year. Hast's Trumpet is soon to follow on the 23rd Day, all these being most Martial. Those born now would do well never to work in a china shop. Cubal's Flame perfectly balances Mr Williams in this third, from 35/3/SY to 34/4/SY both in the Distaff from the start, which is mighty rare and is bound to have some effect. Melok rising towards the house Major is Martial on day 60 when the house Minor which is when Mr Williams comes into the 4th quadrant of Krull. This house is initially Distaff but will wax as The Bull wanes. But Both houses being in the Firmament during the same Third is potent as their occlusion falls on Mid Summer's Day. Then does Old Toesy conjoin with The Void, one being Widdershins, the other Turnwise. Much potency amongst bipeds can be expected, and the nights are long, also. On the 21/4/SY Vut is Martial to Melok and is in harmony with The Void, which is Distaff, so all's well there. The house of Melok wanes into the Distaff by the 50th April (SY) and the house of The Star is seen from Ankh's 4th quadrant, which is a comfort, as now Cubal, The Void, and The Occasional Paddles are at each quadrant of Ankh with that house. Thus this Third ends with Blik-Blick being unaccustomedly Martial.

[67]

Finish of the Common Year

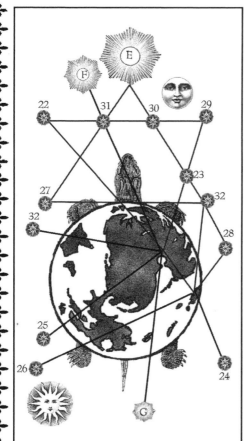

The Celestial Chart showing the stars as they will be after the first 400 Day cycle, perhaps.

This final Third of the Common Year starts with May of the Scholastic Year and ends with Grune on its 16th day, thus making 400 days in total or half the Scholastic Year.

The house of The Star dominates and is Martial.

The BRIGHT CABBAGE

arrives but is not influenced unduly, which is as well.

However the Starfish, which is the named star of the said house, enters the 1st and a quarter quadrant of Ankh and is Distaff from the start.

Whereas

The OLD DOG

rises straight into the 13th quadrant of Krull on the 32nd May (SY) and is Martial.

It is not until

The PITCHER and The LITTLE TURTLE

meet up and align with

The STARFISH and OKJOCK,

all of which are Distaff, that the danger abates, which is as well.

However, it would be well not to be a camel driver during this time.

CRABBUS

is in attendance and Martial from 45th May (SY), just missing the end of the Soul Cake Days. These will be heralded by the new moon on the 35th of the same, and will not have a rain of fish except where the influence of

OLD TOESY

is strongest, and that being Krull, they will go unnoticed.
There is another alignment from

THE PLOUGH HANDLE, OKJOCK, THE LITTLE TURTLE
and THE BRIGHT CABBAGE,

which is unusual even in a half-year ending. Any detrimental influence, which could arise, is negated by the fact that the

HOUSE OF THE PLOUGH

is now ascending by the 58th of May (SY) and that benign presence calms all, although this still causes mischief for redheads in the Brown Islands, but if there are any they are few in number, and soon to get fewer.

The sun has now shifted, but no effect is felt on the Dysc, yet.

THE FLYING MOOSE

has entered on the 6/5/SY and will be seen in the 9th quadrant from Krull, which is nice. Thus The Common Year ends, the Firmament having sustained more alignments than is normally seen though the Astral influences have been muted due to the consanguinity of many of the Stars and Houses.

So we can say, all's well that ends well.

Some notes on Our Celestial Lamp the Moon

Of all the Heavenly Bodies the most beneficial to mankind is without doubt the Moon. Serene and beautiful, like some pale ship sailing across the night sky, it does us much good as well as being an adornment.

The Moon is a most excellent clock, and if not the cause of many surprising accidents, gives just indication of them, and is held to be most efficacious in the planting of pulses and root crops of all varieties. Celery planted at full moon will grow to a height of fifteen feet, whereas potatoes planted under a gibbous moon will explode.

Amongst those who till the soil of the great Sto Plains the sight of a full Moon rising over an ocean of fine growing cabbages is held to be mighty fine and does a man more good than a month of sermons.

The times of the Moon's ebb and flow do also accord a pattern with rain, certainly in the spring. This is also a blessing and does nourish the plants without the vicissitudes of cold and heat that can be found when the Moon is on the wane.

To those brave souls who travel the highways of the Oceans, the Moon is a boon companion, though when rising full over the Rim it has lured many a poor mariner to his death, they following that swan-white path and not their true reckoning. In that there is a lesson for us all.

Some do say that those conceived under a rising moon, and born under a full one, will have much luck and be blessed with beauty if a Maid, and well limbed if a Lad.

The orbits of the Sun and Moon about the World, passing over and beneath it in an ellipse or flattened circle, are very similar and periodically the Moon passes so close to the Sun that one face of it is scorched. By the great foresight of the Keeper of the Geometries, the Moon spins in its path so that this is always the same face, which by now is quite blackened. And thus, when this face revolves towards the world, are the Phases or Aspects of the Moon caused.

The Aspects of the Moon as observed from the Tower of Art at Unseen University, and corroborated by observations made in the Royal Observatory of Krull:

New Moon. When the burnt areas of the Moon are fully presented. Flashes of light seen on the 'dark side' at that time, previously thought to be spirits of some kind, are now known to be nothing more than the exhausts of dragons.

Waxing Crescent. Occurs when the visible Moon is partly but less than one-half illuminated while the illuminated part is increasing.*

First Quarter. When one-half of the Moon appears illuminated, while the illuminated part is increasing.*

Waxing Gibbous. When the Moon is more than one-half but not fully illuminated by direct sunlight while the illuminated part is increasing.*

Full Moon. When the visible Moon is fully illuminated by direct sunlight. There are two Full Moons: **Lunar Majoris (Lumaj)**, when the augmentation of the moon's own light by the sun is at its greatest because the sun and moon are on the same 'side' of the Dysc (this may be seen at sunset or sunrise) and **Lunar Minoris (Lumin)** when the two spheres are on 'opposite' sides.

Waning Gibbous. The Moon is less than fully, but more than one-half, illuminated by direct sunlight while the illuminated part is decreasing.*

Last Quarter. Is when one-half of the Moon appears illuminated while the illuminated part is decreasing.*

Waning Crescent. Occurs when the Moon is partly, but less than one-half, illuminated by direct sunlight while the illuminated part is decreasing.*

* NOTE: It is of some scientific conjecture that this may be due to an increase and subsequent decrease in magical activity within the Moon. There may well be a correlation between this tidal ebb and flow of magical strength and some as yet undiscovered natural phenomenon (the heartbeat of Great A'Tuin itself has been put forward by some scholars). Ed.

Those of us who have studied the ancient texts have observed a most curious and one might say perceptive nomenclature in the seasonal aspects of the Moon's heavenly cycle.

These are as follows:

ICK: THE LONG NIGHT MOON.

OFFLE: THE BLUE MOON.

FEBRUARY: THE HUNGER MOON.

MARCH: THE WAKENING MOON.

APRIL: THE GRASS MOON.

MAY: THE PLANTING MOON.

JUNE: THE ROSE MOON.

GRUNE: THE THUNDER MOON.

AUGUST: THE RED MOON.

SPUNE: THE HUNTING MOON.

SEKTOBER: THE FALLING LEAF MOON.

EMBER: THE ACORN MOON.

DECEMBER: THE PIG MOON.

Memo From Ronald Goatberger, publisher
To: Thomas Cropper, overseer

Mr Cropper, I've been reading the proofs of this. What is a 'groaning chair'?

WITCHES AND THE MOON

There has been some considerable debate about this. Witches are traditionally associated with the Full Moon, but this appears to be for no other reason than that it is easier to get about at this time and there is less peril from unexpected hedgehogs. Contrary to popular opinion, to witches (however Magical it may be in the estimation of wizards, geometers, seers and others) the full moon is no more than a useful light in the sky and a great saving in candles.

However, the two quarter moons, when the moon appears half black and half white, appear to be of some interest to serious witches as a symbol of the truth that a witch's place is between two states (which also explains their attraction to dawns and ducks, deathbeds and groaning chairs and, of course, beaches).

We hear that some witches prefer the gibbous moon because it gives them an opportunity to use the word 'gibbous' in polite conversation. This would be very much in the character of witches.

Memo to Ronald Goatberger
From: Thomas Cropper, overseer

Dear sir, a groaning chair is a chair for giving birth in. Popular in the rural districts, I believe. I imagine it creaks a bit. My old granny told me that there used to be a cake made for the birth and that was called a Groaning Cake. On the posher farms there was even a special cheese made, called the Groaning Cheese. My gran said there was a lot more groaning in the old days, and they were all the better for it.

Memo From Ronald Goatberger, publisher
To: Thomas Cropper, overseer

All right, I understand about the chair. But is a duck a naturally magic bird? I thought witches were more associated with ravens and toads and so on. Ducks, it seems to me, are very un-magical indeed. There is nothing like the quack of a duck to lend a little mundane humour to a situation. This is clear.

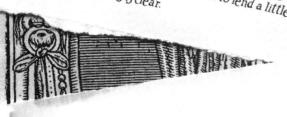

Memo to Ronald Goatberger

From: Thomas Cropper, overseer

You know, sir, you're the first person to point that out since I've been here, and that's more than forty years! Oh dear. If we correct it now, people will notice. They do read the text very closely up in the mountains, when they're in the privy. I suppose they thought it was all right. But don't you worry, sir, we in the almanack trade can rise to any occasion. My lad Zeb will put his mind to it.

The Role of the Duck in High Magic

FEW PEOPLE ARE AWARE OF THE ROLE PLAYED BY THE COMMON DUCK IN THE FOLKLORE AND MYTHOLOGY OF THE WORLD. FOR SOME REASON THERE HAS BEEN A RELUCTANCE TO TALK ABOUT THE LOATHSOME DUCK OF GENUA, WHICH ESCAPED THE POULTERER'S AXE AND TOOK REFUGE IN THE CITY'S SEWERS, WHERE IT GREW ENORMOUSLY FAT ON RATS AND BABY ALLIGATORS AND TERRORISED THE POPULACE WITH ITS FIERY BREATH UNTIL IT WAS KILLED BY MEANS OF AN ORANGE.

PATINA, GODDESS OF WISDOM, IS KNOWN TO BE ACCOMPANIED BY A DUCK AT ALL TIMES, OFTEN WRONGLY REFERRED TO AS A PENGUIN BY THOSE WHO HAVE NOT PROPERLY STUDIED THE ANCIENT TEXTS.

CURIOUSLY WRITTEN OUT OF EARLY LEGENDS ABOUT THE CREATION OF THE UNIVERSE IS THE GREAT DUCK, FROM WHOSE SINGLE EGG THE WHOLE OF CREATION WAS HATCHED. HOWEVER, THE TRUTH WILL OUT, AND IT IS NOW KNOWN THAT, FROM THE OUTSIDE, INFINITY IS DUCK-EGG BLUE.

IN THE MOUNTAINS OF HUBWARD HOWONDALAND, TRIBES BELIEVE IN A GREAT WHITE DUCK, WHOSE FEATHERS FALL AS SNOW, WHICH AT THE END OF TIME WILL NABBLE THE WORLD INTO NOTHINGNESS.

ANNUALLY ON SOUL CAKE DAY, THE GOOD PEOPLE OF THE TOWN OF ÜBERGIGL HOLD 'THE RUNNING OF THE DUCKS', WHEN MADDENED UNTAMED DUCKS RUN, MORE OR LESS, THROUGH THE STREETS OF THE TOWN AND THE YOUNG MEN VIE WITH ONE ANOTHER TO BE THE ONE TO SNATCH THE COVETED ROSETTE FROM THE BEAK OF THE BIGGEST DRAKE.

IN UBERWALD, PEOPLE LIVE IN FEAR OF THE WEREDUCKS, WHICH ARE PERFECTLY NORMAL DUCKS FOR MOST OF THE MONTH BUT DURING FULL MOON BECOME EVEN STUPIDER BUT CONSIDERABLY MORE AGGRESSIVE. TRAVELLERS THROUGH

DAMP AREAS WHO HEAR THE SLAP OF WEBBED FEET BEHIND THEM SHOULD HURRY AWAY AND ON NO ACCOUNT LOOK AROUND. IT IS SAID THE DUCKS ARE VAMPIRES, BUT ALSO THAT THEY ARE LAUGHABLY BAD AT IT.

IT IS CLAIMED BY THE OMNIANS THAT WHEN BISHOP HORN WAS FASTING IN THE DESERT A CHARIOT APPEARED IN THE SKY, DRAWN BY SEVEN TIMES SEVEN WHITE DUCKS, AND IN IT THERE WAS AN ANGEL WITH A SCROLL, THAT CRIED OUT: 'FIVE TIMES FIVE IS THE NUMBER OF THE HOUR, AND A BUSHEL OF WHEAT WILL TURN IT!' THE MEANING OF THIS HAS NEVER BEEN ASCERTAINED, AND IT IS BELIEVED THAT THE ANGEL HAD IN FACT MADE A MISTAKE.

LEGENDS IN THE RAMTOPS TALK OF THE BLACK DUCK THAT WILL TRY TO ENTER THE HOUSE OF THOSE DYING OF EMBARRASSMENT, AND QUACK AT THEM IN A MEANINGFUL WAY.

NO MENTION OF THE IMPORTANT ROLE DUCKS HAVE PLAYED IN MYTHOLOGY WOULD BE COMPLETE, OF COURSE, WITHOUT A MENTION OF THE DUCK OF THE IRON BOOK, WHICH AT THE END OF THE WORLD WILL RISE UP AND UTTER THE QUACK OF DOOM. IT IS SAID TO HAVE SEVEN HEADS, AND ON EACH HEAD SEVEN MORE HEADS, WITH NINE FEATHERS UPON EACH HEAD, AND [continued page 666]

 Make the Hole here

Of Town and Country

A useful compendium of
Facts & Essential Information
Both rural and metropolitan

 Laid before the
readers of this
Publication under the
sponsorship of

The
Ankh–Morpork
and
Wincanton

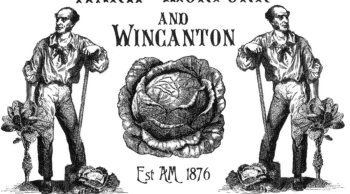

Est AM 1876

Cabbage Growers Association

MARKETS

ANKH-MORPORK

Being the largest and most prosperous City on the Dysc, Ankh-Morpork has innumerable markets.

Some are regulated by the nature of their geography, these being the permanent Butter and Cattle Markets and the Pearl Dock Fish Market. Major markets are held weekly in Sator Square and Whopping Street.

Others are totally peripatetic and can spring up in an instant. Even the inhabitants of the city are unable to predict the next eruption of barrows, hawkers and sellers of all manner of goods. In fact the reason why market carts so frequently have wheels is that in the city some markets actually do move continuously in order to get round an ancient prohibition which assumed that commerce is stationary. Most notable amongst these is the Endless Street Fruit, Vegetable and Ferret market, which circumnavigates the city three times on Thursdays. Many bargains are to be had here by the fleet of foot, and those of a less agile persuasion are advised to learn how to throw coins accurately and perhaps also to invest in a butterfly net to catch the goods.

 DAILY

GENERAL LIVESTOCK: the Cattle Market.

POULTRY: The Goosegate.

HORSES: Upper Broadway, Edgeway Road and Pigsty Hill.

EGGS, BUTTER, CHEESE AND OTHER DAIRY: Hen & Chickens Field, Butter Market and Cheesemongers Yard.

BEEF, PORK, MUTTON, LAMB: Chittling Street Cattle Market, The Cham

RAT MARKET (meat, breeders, yearlings and Fancy): Treacle Mine Road. Other indigenous dwarf foodstuffs are also sold here.

FLEA MARKET (breeders and Fancy): Mr Fakenthorn's tray, outside the Seven Peccadilloes pub, Five and Seven Yard. (Also, in season, venture here for flea circuses and, in the evenings, flea experimental drama and dance.)

FRUIT, VEGETABLE AND GENERAL PRODUCE MARKETS are held most days at Nap Hill, Five and Seven Yard, the Cattle Market and Goosegate.

CART-TAIL SALES are held by the Thieves' Guild on most weekdays, in conjunction with the local markets; these are the places to go to buy back your own goods at very reasonable prices.

 WEEKLY

Sator Square. SATURDAY
Fruit, vegetables, fish, meat, game & other comestibles.
Second-hand clothes, and non-comestibles; magical items sold in the midnight hour.

Whopping Street Market. TUESDAY, FRIDAY, OCTEDAY
Fruit, vegetables, fish, meat, game & other comestibles.
Second-hand clothes, and non-comestibles.

Lobbin Clout Market. OCTEDAY ONLY
Smaller, more local.
Fruit, vegetables, fish, meat, game & other comestibles.

Pearl Dock Public Fish Market. FRIDAY
(There are wholesale markets here at dawn every day.)

MONTHLY

Dragons' Landing.
All comers tinsmith's market.
Metal work, old farm machinery, pots, pans, domestic & commercial.
The Thieves' Guild patrols this market for unlicensed stolen goods.

⇥ QUARTERLY FAIRS ⇤
(Common Year)

These are normally all held on Twitcher Street Green.

MARCH: The Lamb Fair.

All manner of new and leaping livestock, plus woollen goods, and manic preachers glad to get out in the fresh air.

MAY: Spring Fair.

Livestock, but also traditional items and fortune tellers.

SEKTOBER: Soul Cake Fair, and Mop Market.

This is not a Mop market in the traditional sense, where artisans and servants stand in rows holding, or wearing, a token of their occupation. The vibrant nature of Ankh-Morpork's commerce causes the ebb and flow of employment to continue all the year round. But outsiders, who do not know the ways of the 'Big Wahoonie', as the indigenous inhabitants call the city, still find this a useful start to their careers in the capital. As do, we are afraid, every pickpocket, slab-man, cudgeltoff and run-grabber in the city, thus giving the newcomers a lesson in what to expect.

This is also the time of the Soul Cake Days (see calendar) and the three days of the Fair coincide with the three days of the festive holiday.

HOGSWATCH EVE: Goose Fair.

All manner of Hogswatch victuals, mostly Porcine in nature despite the name of the fair, plus gifts, toys, candles, goose grease for children and copious quantities of pickles. Strong drink is much in evidence.

⇥ SPECIALIST FAIRS ⇤

MIDSUMMER: The Tump Horse Fair.

One of the oldest in the world (and the one from which the term 'stump up', meaning to pay right now, derives).

NOVEMBER 1: The Mollymog Candle and Tallow Market.

Mollymog Street. This is held in the evening, by candlelight.
The place for the prudent housewife to buy her year's supply of candles.

There is much drinking of mulled wine and it is said to be the scene of notable debauchery, although we've never been able to get there in time.

NIGHT OF THE FULL MOON: The Assassins' Fair.

Held atop the old bell tower near Five Ways, which is inaccessible to anyone not very familiar with the use of crampon and grapnel. General sale of fine clothing, well-crafted tools, weaponry, maps, information, etc.

NIGHT OF THE NEW MOON: The Unfair (Thieves' Fair).

Held in the crypt of St Front Without The Soake. By custom and practice, this is not limited to members of the Thieves' Guild, and here may be purchased striped jumpers, dark lanterns, coshes, swag bags, domino masks and similar. Stool pigeons and fall guys are generally for hire.

FEBRUARY 12: The Lobbin Clout Pin Market.

It sells pins, there's no getting away from it. If you want pins, pins are here. All types of pins. This is the place where pins may be found. Pins old and new. It is the high spot of the year for people who collect pins. Last year, a very rare Tweedsmill hand-made pin with the trademark recurved head fetched no less than $79.35 at auction. It was a big moment in the pin world, and has caused much discussion wherever 'pinheads', as they laughingly call themselves, foregather to talk pins.

Outside Ankh-Morpork

Chirm
MARKETS (other than local): approximately first Octeday in the Month.
FAIRS: May, August, Sektober, Ick.

Sto Lat
MARKETS: Normally on a Saturday.
FAIRS: May, Sektober, Ick.

Sheepridge
MARKET DAY: Friday.
FAIRS: March, June, Sektober, Ember (Mop Market), Ick.

Sto Kerrig
MARKET DAY: Wednesday.
FAIRS: on Soul Cake Days, Ick.

Sto Helit
MARKET DAY: Octeday.
FAIR: on Soul Cake Day.

Quirm
MARKETS: Wednesday and Saturday.
FAIRS: on Soul Cake Day, Ember (Mop Market), Ick.

Pseudopolis
MARKET DAYS: Wednesday, Friday, Octeday.
FAIRS: May, Grune, on Soul Cake Days, Ick.

A deaf man needn't hear bells to know his house is on fire.

Old Proverb

Rham Nitz

THE EEL MARKET: every Friday, Sektober to February.
FAIRS: Spune (Salmon Fair), Grune, on Soul Cake Days, Ick.

Gebra

MARKETS: All the time, including some which trade in a variety of
products not normally associated with any but a temporary transaction
within the whore pits. To be avoided unless you have a complete working
knowledge of the local language and customs.

Uberwald

There is a sort of mop market in most towns, but employment working
for the gentry is apt to be terminal unless your name is Igor.

THE CABBAGE AND SPROUT FAIR

BIG CABBAGE, STO PLAINS
('THE HEAD OF THE CABBAGE INDUSTRY')

SEKTOBER 1ST–3RD

Here is where cabbage futures are bought and sold, fields of cabbages
as yet un-sown are auctioned, seeds are traded, and events crucial to
the cabbage, sprout and greenstuffs industry are discussed. On the
first day of this three-day market, the CABBAGE QUEEN is crowned.

NOTE: This is new and replaces a number of smaller fairs.

AND REMEMBER EMBER 5TH:
The Big Cabbage Carnival of Kale

ANKH–MORPORK
AND
WINCANTON

Est AM 1876

Cabbage Growers Association

The Grand Provincial President of the Association is pleased to announce that the Councils of all Provincial, Regional and District Sheds have finally agreed to the formal classification of Exhibition & Culinary Brassicas.

At the Annual General Meeting of the Classification Committee, the motion was carried by a majority of 316 to 296.

There were 3 abstentions, 2 duels and 1 sudden death.

The full classification list, along with the detailed specification of each variety and sub-species is now before the General Exhibition Committee, who are forming a working party to formulate the definitive seasonal and aesthetic parameters prior to the submission of data from the Olfactory Committee under the temporary chairmanship of Mr Tweed.

A full report will follow.

The President would like to pass on his thanks to all those members who were able to take part, and offers his condolences to Mrs Wellgroom on the sad demise of her late husband, again.

THE EDITOR is pleased to be able to reproduce here an extract from the

CABBAGE COMPANION

A publication of the Ankh-Morpork Growers Club in collaboration with the STO HELIT BRASSICAS ASSOCIATION.
A silver donation has been made to the Junior Growers Club, the 'Green Nippers', in recognition of this. (Ed.)

Common Cabbage Varieties

Morning Glory
Large, big-hearted variety that grows in wet conditions and is almost resistant to background magic and frogs. Tastes slightly of mice.

Schweinfart Emperor
Rare breed from Uberwald, quite liked by Vampires because werewolves are sickened by the smell.

Jolly Giant
Small but very green, good for soups as it expands in water by three hundred per cent.

Savoloy Special
Named after its original breeder, Mr Harold Savoloy, who was aiming to produce a cabbage suitable for sausage making. The cabbagewurst never caught on, though, because green sausages often don't.

The Kendle Green
A Red Cabbage. Oh, how they laugh at this on the farms of the Sto Plains! Has a hint of mustard.

Titanic Iceberg
Technically a cabbage although the 'head' in fact forms underground, this frost resistant variety is often 14 times larger underground than on top. Large ones have been known to strip the wheels and bottoms of farm carts that try to run over them. A good keeper. The hard part is getting rid of it.

Porraceous Sprouter
A good winter grower, which must be picked before the first full moon of March or it will grow huge inedible leaves within seconds.

Sto Whopper
A variety that grows to a huge size in all weather conditions, and probably a 'sport' from one of the old duelling varieties.

Sto Leafy
A variety that grows to a huge size in all weather conditions, with bigger leaves.

Sto Stout
A variety that grows to a huge size in all weather conditions, but looks fatter from the side.

Sto Stalker
A variety that grows to a huge size in all weather conditions, but seems to follow you home and wait outside the privy at night when you're in there after a good helping of cabbage beer.

Sto Red
A variety that grows to a huge size in all weather conditions, but is really, really green. When they come up with a good joke out there on the cabbage farms, they don't let it go in a hurry.

Micklegreens Juicy
A variety that grows to a huge size in wet conditions, but if you are unfortunate enough to tread near after it is ripe it will explode over you and no amount of scrubbing will get the smell off for weeks.

Helit Prize
A beautiful full-crowned cabbage with a firm heart, full-leaved, easy to grow, almost picks itself, can never be overcooked, but is totally inedible. Sold for export.

Offle King
A white cabbage that is green to look at before cooking; good for salads, beer making and soling shoes.

Blue Bolter
Blue green with a small heart but large outer leaves, very nervous and, owing to some residual magical gene, prone to run away if startled.

Big Hearted Arthur
A cross between the old variety of Askey and a mute hybrid called Mabel. A good money maker.

Burly Bolter
As Blue Bolter, but will leap up out of the ground and head-butt you.

Choi Champion
An aristocrat of cabbages, smooth, urbane, well connected, likes to be planted close together away from any other Brassica. Prone to sneering.

SCENTLESS MUTE
A very quiet variety that is so pungent it will render the picker's olfactory senses useless for days when picked. A good boiler.

SPRING POUNCER
The tightly packed outer leaves have a habit of unfurling when it is picked. This releases the inner leaves which are razor sharp. A good eater, but wear chain mail gloves when picking.

AUTUMN RELIANT
Has to be planted in late summer or it will flower in Sektober. Needs lots of pushing, is prone to rot, but is cheap and easy to grow. Tastes foul, because it is stuffed with vitamins.

KING'S SNIVEL
Ephebian mythology tells us that the cabbage sprang from the fallen tears of a king who was about to be killed by one of the Gods for making water amongst His holy grove of turnips. As the King's tears fell, the god felt compassion and turned him into a tortoise. He was eaten by an eagle five minutes later, but it's the thought that counts.

THE FALSE CABBAGE
Beware! This poisonous plant is not a cabbage at all, but pretends to be one to escape enemies, which shows how clever plants are. Deadly if eaten, but can be neutralized if accompanied by beer.

THE CABBAGE FROG
Again, not a cabbage and not even a plant. It is one of nature's mimics. It grows 'leaves' and remains motionless amongst real cabbages until errant butterflies try to lay eggs on it and then, snap!

INTERESTING CABBAGE FACTS No 324

During one of the many wars that ebbed and flowed over the Sto Plains a group of Pseudopolitan soldiers decided to ambush a detachment of the Sto Militia, (the Cabbidgers). They dug a cunningly concealed slit trench beside the road, covering their heads in cabbage leaves. However the Sto Militia were not as green as they were cabbage looking, and soon planted them for good.

Great Moments In Cabbage History
No. 16

The first recorded cabbage duel was in the Year of the Pensive Frog, on or about Hogswatch, and followed an argument between the chef to Lord Rumptuous and the Head Gardener whereup (according to the *Chronicles of the Sto Plains*) 'Gardener Seth seised him of an fresh Cabbarge lying By and smote the Cook about the head, but Cook evaded the blow right well and, seising also an Cabbidge in both hands, smakèd Seth in the stomach and then brake the cabage in two upon his pate.'

Alas, the cabbage duel, either as a matter of honour or as a sideshow at the local fairs, is now hardly ever seen. For a time it was very popular amongst the gentry of the Plains and strains of cabbage were bred expressly for duelling. However, so far as we know, no one these days grows Old Anchor, which sank in water and could not be cut with a knife, or Red Whammy, which was completely inedible and dangerously explosive if it dried out.

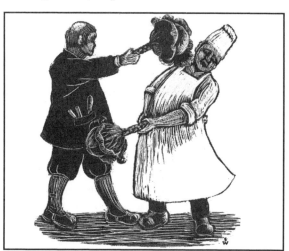

Makepeace Thomas Bounder

known as The Poet of the Cabbages. He was born in humble circumstances in Pop 247, and died there eighty years later in slightly humbler physical circumstances but otherwise amongst the great Muses. (Those unfamiliar with placenames on the Sto Plains might like to know that his home town was originally known as Fork's Bend, but the sign rotted and fell off at least fifty years before Makepeace's birth, leaving on the post only the smaller sign bearing witness to the level of population, which no one bothered to remove or change [the sign, that is. Most of the population removed itself]. By the inexorable force of tradition, Pop 247 is now the official name of the town, known locally as 'Pop'.)

Raised to be a cabbage hoer, Makepeace taught himself to read off old feed sacks and seed packets, and at the age of only fourteen penned perhaps his best-known work, 'Cabbages', written during the great cabbage-root fly epidemic of 1839. Every schoolboy can quote the opening lines:

> I WANDERED LONELY AS A CLOWN
> O'ER SLIMY SCENES OF INSECT MASSACRES,
> FOR THERE THEY LAY AROUND THE TOWN
> A HOST OF SLIMY GOLDEN BRASSICAS...

He wrote more than two thousand poems, all broadly on the subject of green winter vegetables and mostly on the backs of old seed bills, but he was not, as critics say, a man with only one vegetable on his mind, as is evinced by 'Oh, Parsnips!' and another favourite, 'Ode to a Carrot Weighing Three Pounds, Four and One-Quarter Ounces, Upon the Making of a Necessary Stew'. This commemorates his Arthur, a pet carrot that had to be sacrificed to the cooking pot towards the end of the Great Famine of 1868:

THEY CUT YOU UP, MY MUM AND DAD,
THEY DO NOT WANT TO, BUT THEY DO,
FOR ALL THE TURNIPS HAVE GONE BAD,
AND WE MUST MAKE A STEW OF YOU...

He was for the whole of his life a passionate enemy of the potato, which he called 'this Swollen Bag of Dirty Water', and wrote a pamphlet entitled A *Fulmination Against The Hellish Root*, in which he declared: 'Time was when the Honest Working Man would sit down to a Hearty meal of Cabbage in all its Infinite Variety, which supplies all he could want in Generous Proportions and, by encouraging the Copious Venting of the Wind, rids the Body of Bad Humours, but now the Hellish Root numbs him and nails him to his chair.'

Makepeace worked diligently on behalf of the cabbage-growing workers across the plains and his belief in the future of the cabbage and associated vegetables was nothing short of messianic. He wrote: 'Give me but five acres, and I shall show you a man entirely self-sufficient in everything needful. With a little thought, a cabbage leaf can make a very serviceable hat, and a strong if coarse thread can easily be spun from parsnips.'

Towards the end of his life, he devoted his limited income to setting up schemes to make clothing from kale, shoes from carrots and beer from beetroots; repeated failure only spurred him to greater efforts. The clothing never caught on, although he himself wore it on every possible occasion, but the beetroot beer is still brewed wherever no alternative presents itself.

His death by explosion occurred while he was writing his final poem, 'On First Looking Into a Five-Year-Old Barrel of My Best Pickled Cabbage'. There is a podium commemorating him, but there is no statue upon it because he insisted in his will that 'any gravestone or other marker' erected after his death should be made of a cabbage-based concrete of his own devising. One was indeed constructed, but was removed after two years because of the smell. The anniversary of his death is commemorated in Pop every year by people asking 'Who was he, then?'.

Make the Hole here

Makepeace Thomas Bounder, 'The Poet of the Cabbages'

THE
ANKH-MORPORK
AND
WINCANTON

Est AM 1876

Cabbage Growers Association

Consulate Branch.
c\o Room 41
Annex.

For the Notice Board.

JUNE. Guest lecture, "Know your Brassicas"
An illustrated talk by Mr Albert Needle (Chairman of the
Ankh-Morpork Cabbage Fanciers) on 'The Wonderful World of
Brassicas' will be given in the auditorium of the
Consulate on 4th June.
As you are probably aware, June is the Cabbage month on
the Sto Plains, just outside Ankh-Morpork, and to
celebrate the occasion the Ladies of the Ankh-Morpork
Cabbage Chorus will open the proceedings with a few pieces
from their repertoire.
Members are invited to bring along examples of their own
efforts, and there will be a general discussion
afterwards.
My 'better half', Doreen, has made some splendid Cabbage
Jam, which she will be happy for you to partake of.
If the time is available, Mrs Strinburg (Accounts) will
recount her trip to the great Cabbage Fields of Sto, and
show us her pictures of that wonderful landscape.

AUGUST MEETING: "Pickling Cabbage, pitfalls and
procedures".
12th August, in the auditorium, Victor Wadmore (Janitor's
Dept.) will give a talk on Pickling Cabbage, pitfalls and
procedures.
We all remember Vic from last year, his pickled cabbage
won both the Wincanton and the Sto General all comers'
competition, so I'm sure we are all agog to find out about
his latest adventures in this exciting field of Preserving
Brassicas.

SEPTEMBER MEETING
19 September, in the Consulate sports field.
"Coping with Flatulence".
Victor Wadmore (Janitor's Dept.) will give an illustrated
talk on the problem we all sometimes face.
Vic has some novel ideas on coping with the condition, but
will not be demonstrating the more spectacular ones
indoors due to the problems we had last year.
A note from Mervyn, our social secretary: Mrs Clithold,
thanked the Society for the donations towards her glass
eye, and as a way of saying thanks had the iris coloured
cabbage green.

That's all for now, happy growing, and death to the demon
caterpillar eh.

A Fletchgrovel (Sec)

MUSHROOMS.

Save this page and take it with you when hunting.

Pretty Murderer
So deadly that you will come back as a zombie and still be ill.

Handy Cap
Edible

Black Cap
Deadly

Woody Whopper
Edible

Woodland Todger
Edible

Grassy Todger
Edible

False Todger
Inedible

Slippery Eric
Inedible

Cut Here

Maiden's Girdle
Very Edible

Maiden's Blush
Very, very Edible

Old Wives' Surprise
Just Edible

Smutty Top
Edible

Witches' Bonnet
Inedible

Red Topped Leveller
Inedible to deadly, depending on time of year

Shaggy Death Cap
Inedible and very deadly

Permed Death Cap
Deadly

Smooth Death Cap
Inedible and deadly even to look at

 Make the Hole here

Miss Ophelia
Spoonfeeder's
Everlasting
Diary

It is with grateful thanks to Miss Spoonfeeder that the editor lays before you this **Everlasting Diary**.

Her travels amongst the heathen races in search of interesting customs are second only to those of the great Sir Roderick Purdeigh, whose acquaintance she made in Bhangbhangduc shortly before his mysterious disappearance. Her many learned pamphlets and journals on the courtship rituals of the heathen (lit. 'non trouser wearing') are the cornerstone of private collections all over the Dysc and have added immeasurably to scholarship on certain matters. But it is for her 'Everlasting' diary that she will be remembered. This simple formula of structuring the year in its base form and writing on the day in question only in pencil was a stroke of genius.

Miss Spoonfeeder was a staunch member of the Reformed Potato Church. Amongst this congregation all the days of the week are considered far too holy to be represented in any temporal book, or written down by an unbeliever's hand. Therefore a space has been left where the day would otherwise appear, thus adhering to her wishes and belief, and allowing those of a similar persuasion to use this diary without any conflict of conscience.

We trust you will find it an easy and foolproof method of recording events, providing moreover a simple 'aide-memoire' for those occasions which Miss Spoonfeeder has noted in such graphic detail.

Personal Information

This Almanak belongs to:

....

This year my pet name / nom-de-plume / nicked name is:

....

I normally live in / under / on a: ....
The address of which is: ....

....

....

My **Private** Astrological Information	This year my resolutions are: None	Birthdays I must remember

My Private Astrological Information

Krullian named year:............
Scholar's Year: ....
My name for the Year:
....
I was born under the sign of:
....
My perambulate star signs are:
Rising: ....
Ebbing: ....
My Shoe size is:................

This year
my
resolutions
are:
None
....
The same
as last year
....
Other:
....
....
....
....
....
....

Birthdays I must remember
....
....
....
....

Birthdays I must forget
....
....

Anniversaries

If found please return this ALMANAK to
me / my significant other / a parent / sibling /
the City Watch (not Cpl Nobbs)
Mrs Cake

THIS BEING A DREAD MONTH. DON'T WRITE ANYTHING INCRIMINATING

But if you have to, write the day in the space provided

	1	
	2	
	3	
	4	
	5	
	6	
	7	
	7+1	
	9	
	10	
	11	
	12	
	12	
	14	
	15	
	16	

BIRTHDAYS	
FUNERALS	
WEDDINGS	
OTHER	

OFFLE

WRITE THE DAY
(IN YOUR BEST HANDWRITING)
OPPOSITE THE RELEVANT DATE.
YOU MAY IF YOU WISH WRITE
YOUR OWN SPECIAL NAME FOR
THE MONTH HERE.
.... January

DAY — **THINGS TO DO**

	Day		Things to do
	1		
	2		
	3		
	4		
	5		
	6		
	7		
	7+1		
	9		
	10		
	11		
	12		
	13		
	14		
	15		
	16		
	17		
	17+1		

BIRTHDAYS	
FUNERALS	
WEDDINGS	
OTHER	

	19	
	20	
	21	
	22	
	23	
	24	
	25	
	26	
	27	
	27+1	
	29	
	30	
	31	
	32	
	33	
	34	
	35	
	36	

⚔ ANNIVERSARIES & OTHER INTERESTING THINGS ⚔

Plough Monday. This falls on the first Monday of the month

FEBRUARY

WRITE THE DAY
(IN YOUR BEST HANDWRITING)
OPPOSITE THE RELEVANT DATE.
YOU MAY IF YOU WISH WRITE
YOUR OWN SPECIAL NAME FOR
THE MONTH HERE.
....

☞ DAY ☜   ☜ THINGS TO DO ☞

Day		Things to do
	1	
	2	
	3	
	4	
	5	
	6	
	7	
	7+1	
	9	
	10	
	11	
	12	
	13	
	14	
	15	
	16	
	17	
	17+1	

BIRTHDAYS	
FUNERALS	
WEDDINGS	
OTHER	

	19	
	20	
	21	
	22	
	23	
	24	
	25	
	26	
	27	
	27+1	
	29	
	30	
	31	
	32	
	33	
	34	
	35	
	36	

Anniversaries & other interesting things

Fat Lunchtime in Genua.
Falls on the 19th of this month

MARCH

WRITE THE DAY
(IN YOUR BEST HANDWRITING)
OPPOSITE THE RELEVANT DATE.
YOU MAY IF YOU WISH WRITE
YOUR OWN SPECIAL NAME FOR
THE MONTH HERE.
....

DAY		THINGS TO DO
	1	
	2	
	3	
	4	
	5	
	6	
	7	
	7+1	
	9	
	10	
	11	
	12	
	13	
	14	
	15	
	16	
	17	
	17+1	

BIRTHDAYS	
FUNERALS	
WEDDINGS	
OTHER	

DAY		THINGS TO DO
	19	
	20	
	21	
	22	
	23	
	24	
	25	
	26	
	27	
	27+1	
	29	
	30	
	31	
	32	
	33	
	34	
	35	
	36	

ANNIVERSARIES & OTHER INTERESTING THINGS

APRIL

WRITE THE DAY
(IN YOUR BEST HANDWRITING)
OPPOSITE THE RELEVANT DATE.
YOU MAY IF YOU WISH WRITE
YOUR OWN SPECIAL NAME FOR
THE MONTH HERE.
....

☞ DAY ☜		∾ THINGS TO DO ∾
	1	
	2	
	3	
	4	
	5	
	6	
	7	
	7+1	
	9	
	10	
	11	
	12	
	13	
	14	
	15	
	16	
	17	
	17+1	

BIRTHDAYS	
FUNERALS	
WEDDINGS	
OTHER	

	19	
	20	
	21	
	22	
	23	
	24	
	25	
	26	
	27	
	27+1	
	29	
	30	
	31	
	32	
	33	
	34	
	35	
	36	

✦ Anniversaries & other interesting things ✦

12th April CE 1740: 'Libbereto' Jones wrote the opera *Cabbagori il Fumato*, first performed in the Opera House at Ankh-Morpork. The performance was curtailed during the first act when the audience stormed the stage.

24th April CE 1675: Lorenzo the Kind was crowned king in Ankh-Morpork.

MAY

👉 WRITE THE DAY
(IN YOUR BEST HANDWRITING)
OPPOSITE THE RELEVANT DATE.
YOU MAY IF YOU WISH WRITE
YOUR OWN SPECIAL NAME FOR
THE MONTH HERE.
....

👉 DAY 👈 | ❧ THINGS TO DO ❧

Day		Things to do
	1	
	2	
	3	
	4	
	5	
	6	
	7	
	7+1	
	9	
	10	
	11	
	12	
	13	
	14	
	15	
	16	
	17	
	17+1	

BIRTHDAYS	
FUNERALS	
WEDDINGS	
OTHER	

Day		Things to do
	19	
	20	
	21	
	22	
	23	
	24	
	25	
	26	
	27	
	27+1	
	29	
	30	
	31	
	32	
	33	
	34	
	35	
	36	

⚔ ANNIVERSARIES & OTHER INTERESTING THINGS ⚔

In May of the **Year of the Amending Camel**, Jebe Buble led the Slaves' Volt in Ephebe, over redundancies and enforced manumissions, and introduced the term 'volt' ('to vigorously fight against enlightened changes') into the political forum.

9th May, Year of the Startled Vole: the Battle of Crumhorn was held on this day.

JUNE

☞ WRITE THE DAY
(IN YOUR BEST HANDWRITING)
OPPOSITE THE RELEVANT DATE.
YOU MAY IF YOU WISH WRITE
YOUR OWN SPECIAL NAME FOR
THE MONTH HERE.
....

☞ DAY ☞		ᕫ THINGS TO DO ᕬ
	1	
	2	
	3	
	4	
	5	
	6	
	7	
	7+1	
	9	
	10	
	11	
	12	
	13	
	14	
	15	
	16	
	17	
	17+1	

BIRTHDAYS	
FUNERALS	
WEDDINGS	
OTHER	

	Day	Things to do
	19	
	20	
	21	
	22	
	23	
	24	
	25	
	26	
	27	
	27+1	
	29	
	30	
	31	
	32	
	33	
	34	
	35	
	36	

⚔ Anniversaries & other interesting things ⚔

20th June CE 1480: Count Pettigrew Monflathers led the charge of the Obese Brigade in the 1st Battle of Quirm. The Obese Brigade (no man under twenty-five stone) achieved many successes in short downhill charges and were truly unstoppable. Technically they were a cavalry regiment, but carried their horses.

26th June CE 1803: Jethro Humdrummer invented the single action cabbage drill.

☞ WRITE THE DAY
(IN YOUR BEST HANDWRITING)
OPPOSITE THE RELEVANT DATE.
YOU MAY IF YOU WISH WRITE
YOUR OWN SPECIAL NAME FOR
THE MONTH HERE.

....

☞ DAY ☜		∽ THINGS TO DO ∽
	1	
	2	
	3	
	4	
	5	
	6	
	7	
	7+1	
	9	
	10	
	11	
	12	
	13	
	14	
	15	
	16	
	17	
	17+1	

BIRTHDAYS	
FUNERALS	
WEDDINGS	
OTHER	

Day		Things to do
	19	
	20	
	21	
	22	
	23	
	24	
	25	
	26	
	27	
	27+1	
	29	
	30	
	31	
	32	
	33	
	34	
	35	
	36	

ANNIVERSARIES & OTHER INTERESTING THINGS

3rd Grune CE 1688: On this day the Ankh-Morpork civil war started.
4th Grune CE 1688: On this day the Ankh-Morpork civil war stopped.

30th Grune, Year of the Translated Rat: Aloysius Musk, Composer and Cabbage Propagator, born. Musk believed that any musical instrument could be made from vegetables. He achieved some success with his pumpkin drum and carrot flute, and the courgette ocarina is still made on the Plains. The Elderly Running Bean Viola, though stringy, was less than melodious. Musk's *Vegetable Medley* has never yet been played.

AUGUST

☞ WRITE THE DAY
(IN YOUR BEST HANDWRITING)
OPPOSITE THE RELEVANT DATE.
YOU MAY IF YOU WISH WRITE
YOUR OWN SPECIAL NAME FOR
THE MONTH HERE.
....

☞ DAY ☜		☜ THINGS TO DO ☞
	1	
	2	
	3	
	4	
	5	
	6	
	7	
	7+1	
	9	
	10	
	11	
	12	
	13	
	14	
	15	
	16	
	17	
	17+1	

BIRTHDAYS	
FUNERALS	
WEDDINGS	
OTHER	

	19	
	20	
	21	
	22	
	23	
	24	
	25	
	26	
	27	
	27+1	
	29	
	30	
	31	
	32	
	33	
	34	
	35	
	36	

⚜ ANNIVERSARIES & OTHER INTERESTING THINGS ⚜

On 2nd August CE 1754 Erasmus Wand set sail for the Brown Islands in his experimental craft *The Intestinal Explorer*, a sailing barque made largely from pig bladders. The voyage was apparently undertaken to prove a theory; if this was that such a craft would leak and sink within one hundred yards of the harbour mouth, then it was correct.

14th August CE 1905: Makepeace Thomas Bounder, 'The Poet of the Cabbages', died.

Spune

WRITE THE DAY
(IN YOUR BEST HANDWRITING)
OPPOSITE THE RELEVANT DATE.
YOU MAY IF YOU WISH WRITE
YOUR OWN SPECIAL NAME FOR
THE MONTH HERE.
....

Day		Things to do
	1	
	2	
	3	
	4	
	5	
	6	
	7	
	7+1	
	9	
	10	
	11	
	12	
	13	
	14	
	15	
	16	
	17	
	17+1	

BIRTHDAYS	
FUNERALS	
WEDDINGS	
OTHER	

Day		Things to do
	19	
	20	
	21	
	22	
	23	
	24	
	25	
	26	
	27	
	27+1	
	29	
	30	
	31	
	32	
	33	
	34	
	35	
	36	

Anniversaries & other interesting things

On 30th Spune
in the Year of the Notional Serpent
𝕿𝖍𝖊 𝖌𝖗𝖊𝖆𝖙 𝕲𝖔𝖉 𝕺𝖒
spake unto Brutha.

5th Spune CE 1803: Hiram Blowthroat invented the double action cabbage drill & kettle.

SEPTOBER

☞ WRITE THE DAY ☜
(IN YOUR BEST HANDWRITING)
OPPOSITE THE RELEVANT DATE.
YOU MAY IF YOU WISH WRITE
YOUR OWN SPECIAL NAME FOR
THE MONTH HERE.
....

☞ DAY ☜   ☞ THINGS TO DO ☜

Day		Things to do
	1	
	2	
	3	
	4	
	5	
	6	
	7	
	7+1	
	9	
	10	
	11	} SOUL
	12	CAKE
	13	DAYS
	14	
	15	
	16	
	17	
	17+1	

BIRTHDAYS	
FUNERALS	
WEDDINGS	
OTHER	

	19	
	20	
	21	
	22	
	23	
	24	
	25	
	26	
	27	
	27+1	
	29	
	30	
	31	
	32	
	33	
	34	
	35	
	36	

⊲✖ ANNIVERSARIES & OTHER INTERESTING THINGS ✖⊳

25th Sektober 1898: Famous explorer General Sir Roderick Purdeigh's walking stick found hanging from a tree in Bhangbhangduc. Since his main use for the stick was to hit foreigners over the head to attract their attention, he was presumed 'dead owing to a lack of social graces'.

EMBER

WRITE THE DAY
(IN YOUR BEST HANDWRITING)
OPPOSITE THE RELEVANT DATE.
YOU MAY IF YOU WISH WRITE
YOUR OWN SPECIAL NAME FOR
THE MONTH HERE.
. . . .

DAY		THINGS TO DO
	1	
	2	
	3	
	4	
	5	
	6	
	7	
	7+1	
	9	
	10	
	11	
	12	
	13	
	14	
	15	
	16	
	17	
	17+1	

BIRTHDAYS	
FUNERALS	
WEDDINGS	
OTHER	

	19	
	20	
	21	
	22	
	23	
	24	
	25	
	26	
	27	
	27+1	
	29	
	30	
	31	
	32	
	33	
	34	
	35	
	36	

✕ ANNIVERSARIES & OTHER INTERESTING THINGS ✕

On 22nd Ember CE 1837 Captain Horatio Fanfare of the Selachii Middleweight Mounted Interlopers ascended the Mutterhorn, the highest peak in the Carrack mountains, in the company of his batman and quartermaster, Sidney 'Shopper' Lucy.

5th Ember: Carnival of Kale, Big Cabbage.
Don't miss the tableau of Great Moments In The History of Root Vegetables, which has on occasion led to a riot that had to be broken up by the Watch.

DECEMBER

WRITE THE DAY
(IN YOUR BEST HANDWRITING)
OPPOSITE THE RELEVANT DATE.
YOU MAY IF YOU WISH WRITE
YOUR OWN SPECIAL NAME FOR
THE MONTH HERE.

DAY		THINGS TO DO
	1	
	2	
	3	
	4	
	5	
	6	
	7	
	7+1	
	9	
	10	
	11	
	12	
	13	
	14	
	15	
	16	
	17	
	17+1	

BIRTHDAYS	
FUNERALS	
WEDDINGS	
OTHER	

	19	
	20	
	21	
	22	
	23	
	24	
	25	
	26	
	27	
	27+1	
	29	
	30	
	31	
	32	
	33	
	34	
	35	
	36	

⚜ Anniversaries & other interesting things ⚜

10th December CE 1803: Loquacious Merryman invented the reciprocating cabbage drill, kettle and harmonium.

30th December CE 1880: Death of Lady Amelia Slathers, founder of the Ankh-Morpork Temperance League and the first person to request in her will that she be embalmed in cocoa.

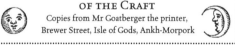

THE
FEARNAUGHT
SOLESAVER

SIMPLY CUT OUT
THIS SHAPE AND INSERT
INTO SHOE OR BOOT,
ONCE LOCATED
IN POSITION
THE
FEARNAUGHT
PATENT
SOLESAVER
WILL PROVIDE
MILES OF
PEDESTRIAN
PLEASURE,

THE FEARNAUGHT SOLESAVER

SIMPLY CUT OUT
THIS SHAPE AND INSERT
INTO SHOE OR BOOT.
ONCE LOCATED
IN POSITION
THE
FEARNAUGHT
PATENT
SOLESAVER
WILL PROVIDE
MILES OF
PEDESTRIAN
PLEASURE.

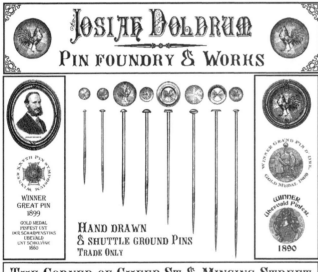

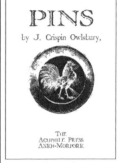

TERRY PRATCHETT is the acclaimed creator of the bestselling Discworld series. 2004 sees the twenty-first anniversary of Discworld, and the publication of *Going Postal*, the thirty-fourth novel of the sequence. He was appointed OBE in 1998.

BERNARD PEARSON, the Cunning Artificer, lives in the town of Wincanton, Somerset, which was recently twinned with Ankh-Morpork.

TRANSWORLD PUBLISHERS
61–63 Uxbridge Road, London W5 5SA
a division of The Random House Group Ltd

RANDOM HOUSE AUSTRALIA (PTY) LTD
20 Alfred Street, Milsons Point, Sydney, New South Wales 2061, Australia

RANDOM HOUSE NEW ZEALAND LTD
18 Poland Road, Glenfield, Auckland 10, New Zealand

RANDOM HOUSE SOUTH AFRICA (PTY) LTD
Endulini, 5a Jubilee Road, Parktown 2193, South Africa

Published 2004 by Doubleday
a division of Transworld Publishers

Printed in Great Britain by Mackays of Chatham plc

1 3 5 7 9 10 8 6 4 2
Papers used by Transworld Publishers are natural, recyclable products made from wood grown in sustainable forests. The manufacturing processes conform to the environmental regulations of the country of origin.